Operation:
BLUE
CHRISTMAS

BASED ON THE REAL LIFE
EXPERIENCES OF A GROUP OF
NEW YORK CITY POLICE OFFICERS

David & Victoria Siev

Operation: Blue Christmas

Printed in the United States of America.

1st Edition – June 2010

ISBN: 978-0-578-05390-5

Cover illustrations: Damon "Sarge" Martin
Cover Christmas constellations: Tomiko, Yumiko and Victor Siev
Book design: Rosamond Grupp

DEDICATION

For all police officers who—remembering duty and forgetting the fear in their hearts—have rushed into the fray.

For all police officers who—forgetting duty but remembering their hearts—have done the right thing.

For every child who refused to take what they see with their eyes as the truth, and dared to look with their hearts.

And to all the dreamers out there, because Hope knows: for those that have changed the world—they were at one time, only a dreamer.

Chapter One

Flashbacks in Blue

The sergeant looked down at the large brown ring surrounding the empty tub. The scalding hot water dripping out of the faucet directly contradicted the bitter cold just outside the window. Down in the street, emergency lights broke through the darkness. Inside the ambulance a little girl lay wrapped in a blanket, shivering from cold, heat and pain. It was a week before Christmas, and the scene was one of the hundreds of jobs called into 911 that night.

* * * * *

I sat with him by our tree as he looked through a batch of letters on Christmas Eve. At work he was a lieutenant in the police department, but at home he was my husband, and father to our children. Every year the letters captivated him—he shook his head on some, smiled and nodded on others. Occasionally he stopped on one or another to think. The usual abundance of energy and nerves that marked this night was gone. For the first time in years, there would be no work for him tomorrow.

Although my husband was sad, nothing could stop the little lights that twinkled in his eyes. Maybe it was because I knew him so well, but his eyes were like movie screens to me. I could always see the scenes through his eyes whenever he told me a story. Now sitting silent, looking over his letters, those screens still lit up with memories in his mind. Over the years of his police career, and of Christmases past, they were all, flashbacks in blue.

There were two cops in full uniform, dancing away in the police station. There was a captain who ended up with coffee all over his shoes. There was a hungry young boy, who's promise to the stars was later kept by a young police officer. And of course, there was the little girl who started the Blue. The magic of the Blue starts with her pain and courage, and makes tough Brooklyn cops act like they were elves. Now, does this all sound farfetched to you?

* * * * *

Fairy tale stories have their own way of starting. Magical stories, about places so far away, they might have never existed. In times unreachable by any of our memories. Heroes and mythical creatures conquering all odds. Way outside the realm of big cities and rough neighborhoods.

But magic still happens. Even in New York. Real magic, where regular people do the best they can, with the little they have. It's not the prettiest thing you've ever seen. Nothing's bright and shiny, nothing's sugar-coated. But it's as real as it gets. And it's still magic. So there you are.

In a land, not too far away, during a time, that wasn't so long ago — an invisible hand stole a tear from a little girl's cheek and placed it inside a policeman's heart. Once upon a time, there was a Blue Christmas.

Chapter Two

Family Christmas

Our four children stormed our room with no regards to the proper amount of sleep. It was Christmas morning of 1998. We followed them to the tree as they laughed and giggled.

Our two middle girls tried to sort the presents into different piles. But the baby boy grabbed everything he could, driving them crazy. Angelina, the eldest, mediated the disputes.

Angelina smiled and repeated everything for her baby brother, Victor. She had a good handle on his antics. The two middle sisters, Tomiko and Yumiko, also repeated themselves. But they believed.

At the age of seven months, Victor spoke one, and only one, word. He had it mastered.

"Victor, these are your presents."

"Huh?"

"Victor. These are your presents."

Everyone believed he understood. And so they repeated themselves. One word was all Victor needed to hold a meaningful conversation.

Victor spoke to everyone. Butting in wasn't a problem either. Maybe people marveled that a baby seemed to understand them, and wanted to hear their voice again. Maybe they liked it that someone was actually listening. Or maybe like his sisters, they believed he almost understood them—so they should just repeat themselves one more time.

Victor's one-word conversations popped up everywhere. Even foreigners fell for his little trick. They smiled and repeated whatever Victor asked for, in whatever language they were speaking.

While Victor's baby-talk intrigued almost everyone, I wondered how the strangers Victor talked to would take to the full-grown version that was his father. A policeman friendly to the point of intrusion, smiling in their faces, asking questions—expecting answers.

"No Victor, *this* is your pile, not that one."

"Huh?"

"No Victor, this is your pile, not *that* one."

Tomiko and Yumiko's efforts met with little success. Finally Angelina grabbed the baby and tickled him so they could finish their task.

* * * * *

The children played with their toys for the rest of the morning. There wasn't one argument for at least an hour. After an early dinner Dave got dressed to leave. He was a sergeant in the NYPD and work didn't stop for holidays.

Before retiring, I had done ten years in the NYPD as a police officer myself. All officers expect not to get holidays off. Not that Dave would have taken tonight off anyway: his evening included a very special mission, which included visiting a certain little girl. Nothing would keep him away from Brooklyn tonight. I grabbed his coat and walked him to the door.

"Will Johnny Mack and Trish help you, Dave?"

Johnny Mack was a policeman I had met several times. His hair seemed red, copper or gold, depending on the light. Something out of his Scottish heritage made his greenish eyes sparkle when he smiled. I heard they glowed when he was angry.

Trish Carlton was the central female figure in Dave's precinct. She was a twenty-something, pretty girl, who wore her blond hair in a spikey style. Most of the policemen in the precinct were only too happy to compete for her attention. If ever she needed something, all she had to do was blink.

"My elves will be there, Vicky. Ready to go."

Chapter Three

Elf School

The drive from our house in Ozone Park, Queens to the 67th Precinct of Brooklyn, was about seven miles, or twenty minutes. Less traffic on the Christmas holiday made the ride a little shorter.

In most big cities, a twenty-minute drive is all you needed to exit one world, and enter another. Ozone Park is a typical middle class neighborhood. Mostly single-family homes, placed closely together on every block.

Dave got to the 67th precinct by getting promoted to sergeant in the summer of 1998. The 67 ("six-seven" in the police world) had a reputation. It was an "A-house," or a "heavy house," meaning heavy in crime. In Brooklyn the six-seven covered all of East Flatbush, and a small part of Brownsville.

Driving through it, you wouldn't know that the precinct was such a heavy house. It was a residential neighborhood, filled mostly with two-family homes, two or three stories high. There were some apartment buildings, and a few store-lined, commercial streets.

Cops who patrolled the six-seven knew the neighborhood to erupt. They weren't sure where or when, but they knew it was coming. Because it always did. A couple of places were rougher than others.

In its southwest corner, the six-seven held the Vanderveer Estates, a complex of fifty-eight buildings, all six stories in height. The "Veer" was considered a high-crime area by its residents, by its neighbors, by the police who patrolled them, and by federal crime statistics.

About fifty or so years ago, you might have seen a teen-aged Barbara Streisand strolling through the Vanderveer Estates. That same walk today might get you mugged. Times change.

* * * * *

The NYPD divided the borough of Brooklyn into the patrol boroughs of Brooklyn North and South. Brooklyn North was filled with A-Houses. Brooklyn South had less, but a heavy house was a heavy house. The hard reputation of the six-seven was well earned.

What Dave didn't know at the time, was that the six-seven was secretly a school for elves. Well, no one knew.

The transition from a civilian, to rookie officer, to a veteran of a heavy house groomed the same characteristics that Dave would need from his elves.

Real elves needed humor, to joke with those who prodded them; neighborhood knowledge, to work their magic accordingly; strong will, to always do right; and strong hearts, so they could lie to little children.

The Blue Christmas operations in the years to come were all about getting in the trenches. There was no writing a check to charity and walking away. Dave would use real elves, to handle real work.

* * * * *

As a rookie sergeant, Dave worked patrol on the four-to-twelve shift, or the third platoon. They were known as the elite patrol officers of Brooklyn South, because they handled the busiest shift, in its busiest precinct. Like the guys he worked with, Dave was a little rough around the edges. As a transit cop, he had worked the train tunnels of the city;

and as a patrol cop, he had worked in Brooklyn North. He had also done some boxing. It was a natural fit when he took Johnny Mack as his driver.

Chapter Four

The Hero's Secret

In the olden days heroes were pitted against fortified castles, evil warlords, dragons—things like that. The few who knew the secret called upon their strength from within. To face any and all odds. But as it was passed up to modern day Brooklyn, those few that understood *the secret* found less and less tyranny to stand up against.

Nowadays *the secret* was about standing up for rights here and there, and keeping a sense of humor. The bold cops of Brooklyn? Let's face it, unless you're slaying dragons, no one wants to hear about the hero-stuff.

✻ ✻ ✻ ✻ ✻

Dave joined the six-seven in the sweltering heat of August, 1998. Over the next few months the hectic work pace quickly forced him to learn his new job. Johnny Mack's knowledge was a big help.

"How's your new driver, Dave, that Johnny McGregor?" I asked him.

"He's not new, Vicky, I am," said Dave. "Good cop, showing me the ropes. A little mischievous—interesting guy though."

"Is that good or bad, Dave?"

✻ ✻ ✻ ✻ ✻

On all precinct matters the buck stopped with its commanding officer, or the "C.O." The highest rank in the precinct was the C.O., working his way up from Captain, to Deputy Inspector, and then finally to Inspector. Another captain acted as a second—the executive officer, or "X.O."

The six-seven's C.O., Inspector Darren McFadden, was a tall, slim, balding man in his early fifties. His desk was organized, his files neat and orderly. He liked to store things away into the black and white cubicles of his mind. Scenarios that didn't fit—he simply chose to ignore. Gray was his least favorite color.

Twenty-five years within the police department had taught McFadden to run a tight ship. He knew policing as a hard and dangerous line of work. He liked it when his staff cringed a little at the sight of him. All ranks needed a healthy fear of their superiors; those without it were not to be trusted.

Johnny Mack wasn't afraid of anyone, or anything. He smiled when the work was easy. He smiled when the work was hard. He never complained. He had a knack of finding evidence at crime scenes; wanted criminals throughout the precinct. Johnny Mack knew the six-seven, and he knew police work. He also understood the secret.

All the bosses in the six-seven liked Johnny Mack, which made McFadden trust him even less.

McFadden once made the mistake of wishing out loud that a lieutenant would leave the six-seven. Lieutenant Roscoe Sardino was too pushy, too nit-picky. He got nothing done. The cops didn't like Sardino at all. It was one of the few times that the C.O. agreed with his men. His wish had been made in earshot of one Johnny Mack.

To the C.O.'s pleasant surprise, Sardino soon asked for a transfer. It was like magic.

Actually, Sardino's wife requested him to leave. Sardino had lost his paycheck in a precinct poker game. She told her husband that he didn't need to work in a place like that. C.O. McFadden signed Sardino's request with the slightest hint of a smile. Inside he was laughing. All who play the game have to lose sometimes. How could a man let his wife push him around so easily? Oh well.

Just as the C.O. was about to change his mind on Johnny Mack, the phone calls started to come in. It was Sardino's wife, with lots of questions. What kind of precinct was the C.O. running? What was his policy on gambling? Did this policy apply to precinct parties? Why were there parties, anyway? What was there to celebrate? Was Johnny Mack a policeman, or a card shark? She called him at least thirty-seven times. Every day.

Sardino's wife then called internal affairs. The New York State Lottery Commission. Gambler's Anonymous. The local senator. Then somehow, she had got hold of the phone number of McFadden's own mother. Whoever she called, in turn called the C.O. The calls never stopped. McFadden knew from the bottom of his heart that any favor he got from Johnny Mack was a curse.

Darren McFadden, the six-seven precinct C.O., made sure to tell his new sergeant that he should keep an eye on that Johnny Mack.

* * * * *

Sometimes heroes might start with saving smaller holidays first. Starting off by saving Christmas is a huge task. Besides, policemen have to work all year long.

"We gotta go to this job over here, Sarge."

"Why Johnny? It's just a dispute."

"Yeah, for the fourth time in the last hour, lets see why it keeps coming over."

On the night before Thanksgiving, Dave and Johnny Mack responded to Church Avenue and East 40th Street. They found a sector car at the scene with a big man and a short woman. One look showed a couple of addicts were in an argument.

"He hit me! He hit me! He's gotta go to jail!"

A very short woman with worn, tight jeans was screaming to an officer. The right side of her face twitched with anger. She was thirty-something, but her height made her look younger. Her eyes were dark and bright at the same time. During the short intervals when she wasn't yelling her face flashed back to a bright smile. Even after years of hard living, Cindy was still a pretty girl.

The object of Cindy's anger was a man in his late forties. His thick beard met his short afro somewhere around his ears without a break. He looked like he had a tire around his face.

The bearded man was holding a big trash bag full of cans. His breath smelled of liquor.

Officer Nicky Adams was speaking to the short lady, but she wasn't satisfied.

"You guys call the police all the time for this. You really have to stop," Adams said.

Johnny Mack pulled the less experienced cops out. "Hey Adams," he called out, "why don't you and Rex come over here and stand with Sarge for a second. Let me talk to them."

Johnny Mack looked at Dave and said, "Sarge, let me handle this, they're regulars." Dave nodded.

The two officers, Adams and Rex, came over by their sergeant. They were a Mutt n' Jeff team: the shorter Adams being a frisky sort, while Rex was tall and slow. Dave looked up at Rex. He imagined that Officer Sturgent was nicknamed "Rex" for the tremendous size of his head.

They both gave Dave a mock fighting stance. Dave was playful, and tended to punch his cops in their arms when he said, "hello." Adams and Rex joked in their fighting stances, but they were mindful of Dave's punches. They attributed Dave's quirks as the result of being punched in the head. Too many times.

"So what's up?" Dave asked the two.

"Get ready for a Johnny Mack special, Sarge," Adams said with a grin.

"Which is?"

"Don't know exactly Sarge. But he'll get this business over with."

After a short chat with the two feuders, Johnny Mack came back. He had a canary-eating grin on his face, and rubbed his hands together.

"This is going to be good," Johnny Mack said.

As he spoke the couple faced off in the middle of the street. They made threatening gestures and started to circle each other. Dave looked at Johnny Mack and raised his eyebrows.

"Don't worry Sarge, these two fight all the time," he said. "Cindy's mad at Mo, but she really doesn't want him arrested."

"That's true Sarge," said Adams. "The desk doesn't want these two in the station house any more. All they do is get each other locked up all the time and then they don't press charges. It's a waste of everyone's time, and it'll ruin their Thanksgiving. They're not real perps (perpetrators of crimes) anyway. "

"Yeah," continued Johnny Mack, "Cindy just wants to get back at Mo."

Now the two were in the middle of the street. Each one of them moved their bodies in a rhythmical manner, gearing up for combat.

Johnny Mack explained to Dave, "Cindy agrees to stop calling 911 if she can get one swing at Mo."

Dave was incredulous. "They're *agreeing* to one swing, Johnny?"

"Yeah, Mo says she couldn't hit him with both his hands down. Says he used to be a boxer."

Dave's eyes lit up, "A *boxer*?"

Dave looked at the two and sure enough Mo was doing a clumsy foot shuffle in front of Cindy. He shook his shoulders and mumbled trash talk.

As she circled Mo, Cindy was working on a swaying rhythm of her own. Like she was about to jump into a double-dutch. Mo was twice her size, but she was clearly angrier.

Suddenly Cindy dipped to the side. She wound up with her left hand, jumped forward, and stopped. Mo fell for the feint. Hook, line, and sinker. He stepped away to avoid Cindy's punch.

Then SMACK! Cindy met Mo's move with her open right hand. The vicious slap spun Mo halfway around.

"Awww!" All four cops yelled at once. It was quite a shot.

The hit brought Mo right out of his drunkenness.

"I'm going to kill her!" Mo yelled. "No one hits Mo like that! She set me up!"

Cindy came running.

"Oooh! I wanna press charges," she said, "he's threatening to kill me!"

But within a couple of minutes Johnny Mack had the two of them calmed down, and holding hands.

Mo admitted that he should have blocked Cindy's slap. It was that hard liquor that had slowed his reflexes. That same evil spirit was the cause of their problems. Because without the drink in him, Mo would never fight with Cindy... she was his love.

Cindy was completely calm now. Her bright smile and pretty eyes showed no malice. She had been vindicated. At that point Dave made an observation of his own. Over the years those pretty eyes must have broken many hearts, the most poignant being that of her mother's.

Cindy and Mo thanked Johnny Mack endlessly. He had made Mo see the error of his drinking ways, and saved their holiday—and their relationship as well. They loved him for that. He was indeed, their hero.

To this Johnny Mack responded that if they called 911 again, he would come back and take their big bag of cans they spent all day collecting.

But they weren't worried about that... because they were back in love.

Back in the police car Johnny Mack observed Dave looking intently at the couple. He read this wrong and asked, "What? You want Rex and Adams baby-sitting those two all night, or do you want them answering real jobs?"

"Excuse me?" Dave snapped back.

"Yeah Sarge, you looked like you were going to ask a question."

"I was Johnny… was that guy Mo really a *boxer*?"

One couple managed to walk away from a fight without the handcuffs. Four cops got to drive away laughing. Brooklyn rules prevailed: no harm, no foul. Thanksgiving was saved.

* * * * *

"Is that the way sergeants supervise jobs in Brooklyn South, Dave?" I asked him that night in bed.

"I don't know, Vicky. It just happened before I knew it. They didn't call 911 again, I know that. Later we responded to an armed robbery that tied us up for the night. I'm glad we got those two out of the way."

"Dave, you know what?"

"What?"

"You're *crazy*."

Many people call the police over trivial matters, slowing down response time to real emergencies. Johnny Mack had handled this problem in a way I've never heard of before. I didn't want to encourage him, but I couldn't stop laughing when Dave got out of bed and reenacted the fight scene between Cindy and Mo.

Chapter Five

A Blue Night

New York City winters can be rough. Enormous swings of temperature, short periods of time. Just below freezing might not be bad, but try that after a spring-like day. When the study comes out linking insanity to violent swings in weather, New Yorkers will already be in the know.

And if you thought that New York City winters don't get that cold, you'd be mistaken. Two degrees Fahrenheit, with a wind chill of minus ten, could be any winter day in the city. As it was that night.

* * * * *

Two cops, a sergeant and his driver, rolled through the streets of Brooklyn. Constantly getting in and out of the car was aggravation. Turn the heat up too much, and it's that much colder when you get out. But when you get back in, you want to get the chill out of your bones. Always looming was the possibility of your next call… which could have you indoors with the heat blasting, while you melted by the minute; or out in the street, getting to understand the true meaning of wind-chill, as you lost all feeling in your toes.

Inside the car, the radio voice of the central dispatcher gave out jobs to the six-seven, and two other precincts. The different sectors replied back to "Central."

Central was the immaculate professional. Central, any Central, could handle ten jobs in three different precincts at the same time.

When handling less than twenty jobs, Central sounded bored. The radio dispatchers of the NYPD were famous for their proficiency.

On a cold December night in 1998, Dave and Johnny Mack were called to respond to a 911 job.

"Six-seven patrol sergeant, on the air?" Central's voice came over the radio.

Dave grabbed his radio, keyed the microphone and responded, "Seven-sergeant. On the air."

"Seven-sergeant, Seven-Adam is requesting you to the location of their aided."

"Seven-sergeant read, show me responding, Central."

"Ten-four, Sarge. I show you enroute."

Sector AB, or "Adam-Boy," or just "Adam" for short, was comprised of Officers Patricia Carlton and Kenny Martin. Trish and Kenny had responded to a radio-run of an aided: a person in need of medical aid. A child had been injured. The circumstances weren't normal, so they called for a sergeant. Dave and Johnny Mack responded.

Sector Adam was in front of an apartment building by Rutland Road, in Brownsville, Brooklyn. It was a five-story walk-up. There were apartment buildings on each of the four corners of East 92 Street and Rutland Road. Small businesses packed the rest of Rutland Road, private houses filled East 92 Street.

An ambulance was already on the scene, its turret lights spanned off rays of red and white into the night. Kenny was in the ambulance writing a report. A little girl about six years old lay wrapped in a blanket. Tears ran down her face as she shivered helplessly. She was clearly in shock. Her mother looked to be in her early thirties, dressed in pajamas and an overcoat. She was an emotional wreck.

"What'cha got, Kenny?" Dave asked.

"Kid's burned bad, Sarge. Fell in a tub—a freak accident." Kenny was writing down something on paper. "Her dad and siblings are upstairs."

The general public has no idea what to do in these situations. Minds shut down as people look for help. Victims of tragedy let authorities take over willingly. Parents of injured children look for the guidance. And it is precisely at this time, when these professionals look for signs of child abuse.

Without saying a word Dave and his cops knew that they were in the middle of a possible child abuse investigation. The first concern was medical aid for the little girl. The next concern was figuring out what had exactly happened.

Dave gave the medic a questioning look. The emergency medical technicians, "EMT's" were the experts.

"We've got to take her to the burn unit at Cornell," he said. He looked at the girl's mother. One of her hands was holding the child, the other was over her face.

"Not good," he mouthed.

Dave made a quick assessment. Choosing the burn unit over the local emergency room meant serious injury. This was no time to speak to the mother. The ambulance had to go from Brooklyn to Manhattan quickly. They had to get the little girl on her way.

"Get the particulars upstairs, Kenny," Dave said. And then to the EMT, "okay, so you guys are out?"

"Just as soon as my partner comes back down," answered the EMT. "He's taking the temperature of the water upstairs."

Dave nodded, "Okay."

Dave and Kenny walked up to the fourth floor apartment. Trish and Johnny Mack were already upstairs. Dave guessed that the building dated back to the twenties, luxurious when it was first built. Now, even with its large, roomy accommodations, it was just another run-down building in a rough neighborhood.

Inside the apartment Trish held the burned girl's younger sister, who looked to be about four. The father sat on a chair with an infant sister, and a boy about two, both on his lap. The father was in his early forties, unshaven, dressed in pajamas. Nothing unusual for a Sunday night.

Dave noted that Trish had separated the father from the four year old. These two would be the only witnesses able to speak, and they had to be separated. Trish had been right to go to the apartment, letting her junior partner fill out the paperwork in the ambulance. It was time to check the accident scene.

Dave walked into a white, old-fashioned bathroom. The fluorescent light was too bright, hurting Dave's eyes. Most of the octagon tiles in the floor were cracked. It was hard to tell what was dirty, or just falling apart. The cracked, white walls had been painted over many times.

Johnny Mack was already there, along with the second EMT. Dave looked down at the empty tub and the dripping faucet. Steam went up as drops of water came down. Instinctively he went to turn off the faucet. The heat made Dave pull his hand back. He put on his gloves to give it another try, but Johnny Mack stopped him.

"It's broken, Sarge," he said, "dripping like that all day."

The EMT nodded his head in agreement.

"How'd the girl get burned?" Dave asked.

The EMT pointed to a wet sock on the floor. "That got stuck in the drain and the tub filled up," he said. A wet broom told the story of how the sock got out. "She fell in the tub playing tag with her brother and sister."

The hot faucet, the endless drip, the sock, the deep tub, the kids playing—and the little girl downstairs. Dave understood, and the image was graphic.

Dave looked again into the white tub. It was one of those big, old-fashioned, cast iron tubs. Real big, real deep. He immediately thought to himself that thank god she didn't go in headfirst.

"What's with the brown ring, was the water dirty?" Dave asked. But when he saw Johnny Mack's face grimace a little, he already wished he hadn't asked.

"That's the skin off her legs," the EMT said. "The water measures out at about one hundred eighty degrees. Her skin just melted off."

He started to explain more, but Dave's waving hand stopped him.

"Okay, I'm going," the EMT said, "need anything else, Sarge?"

Dave looked at Johnny Mack, who shook his head. Dave looked at the EMT and shook his head as well.

Back in the apartment Dave took a quick look around. There were certain things to be done. If a crime had been committed it was up to them to investigate.

Trish was with the four-year old, the only sibling that had any understanding of her sister's condition. She was still too young to know how bad it was, but she remembered how her sister screamed. She held tightly onto Trish, who squeezed her back and patted her hair. Dave imagined that some day Trish would make a good mother.

Johnny Mack went to the father and the two other kids. There was no mischief in Johnny Mack's eyes. He helped the man but allowed space. The two smaller siblings didn't understand a thing. Johnny Mack held the baby while the two year old played with the officer's flashlight. The father was getting dressed.

Kenny looked in the fridge, and in the kid's room. Dave took a look around as well. After five minutes Dave got his cops together. He needed to hear what his cops had found. The father was in another room, dressing his kids to leave.

The situation was delicate, so Dave had sent the junior officer only to look at the concrete facts. He nodded at Kenny to report.

"Food in the fridge, Sarge. The kid's room is sloppy, but there are enough clean clothes around."

Dave agreed. There was food in the house. The apartment wasn't going to win any awards for cleanliness, but it wasn't filthy. Sloppy and filthy were two different things. A filthy apartment without food equaled neglect. Very filthy—or bruised up kids—equaled arrest.

Trish reported next.

"A game of tag, Sarge. The kids were running around the apartment while the parents were watching TV. The game got into the bathroom, the little ones pushed passed their big sister. She fell into the tub."

"How does the four-year old look?" Dave asked.

"She doesn't know how hurt her sister is. She's healthy enough. Well-fed, no signs of bruises."

"Is she going to be all right?" Dave asked.

"I think she'll be okay," answered Trish. "She understands, but doesn't."

Dave nodded. In the station house Trish was all woman. She could flirt, and flash her smile. Out on the streets she was all cop.

Dave then looked to Johnny Mack, who had taken the father.

"The father says the same thing," Johnny Mack said, "and no marks on the little kids either."

Johnny Mack knew that Dave had to make a decision, and he measured his boss the same way Dave measured him. If you looked deep enough into Johnny Mack's eyes, you'd see the green hills of his ancestors.

The initial police investigation was complete. Trish, Kenny and Johnny Mack all looked to the sergeant. It was his call. What happened next was on Dave.

Dave knew that the Administrative Children's Services, ACS, would come into the picture later with a style of their own. They would interview, re-interview, watch, and re-watch the whole family. ACS would be sure to continue with the parents. They would go over the whole family with rights and wrongs of raising their children.

"This is a bad accident, nothing else," Dave said. He looked at Trish and told her, "Mark this job as an aided going to the burn unit."

Kenny, Trish, and Johnny Mack all breathed out a sigh of relief. If Dave called it a possible child abuse, the investigation would have started immediately. The family would be taken into police custody. ACS and Special Victims Detectives would be called to the precinct that night. Hours of interviewing would start as soon as they came. The parents would lose their children that night, and their plight would go from nightmare, to demonic.

Over the radio six-seven Edward asked for permission to go to meal, but Central was still holding jobs in the six-seven. A sector couldn't take a meal while their precinct was holding 911 jobs. Central denied the meal to the sector, and then dished out four jobs to the neighboring precinct without taking a breath.

Trish waited for a space to talk, then keyed her radio. "Six-seven Adam to Central," she said.

"Seven Adam."

"Mark this job. An aided to the Cornell burn-unit, via ambulance."

"Ten-four, Adam. Sector Eddie is looking for meal."

"What are you holding, Central?"

"Holding a dispute on Farragut and Troy—corner of; and a past larceny of cigarettes at Rite-Aid, Albany and Church."

"Give me both jobs, Central. Tell Eddie to enjoy their meal." She smiled weakly at Dave and Johnny Mack, "Kenny and I could use something to do."

Kenny nodded in agreement.

A gruff voice came over the radio, "Eddie read direct, thank you Adam."

Trish looked back at her four-year old friend before walking out. The little girl was sad to see her go.

"You leaving, Police?" she asked.

Trish bent down to speak to the little girl. "I have to go sweetie," she said. "But I got a job for you."

"What's that, Police?"

"You share this with your father and brother," she handed the girl a pack of life-savers, "and help your father with your brother and sister tonight. Okay?"

The little girl didn't want to see Trish leave, but she nodded bravely. Then, with her best smile and a wink, the policewoman was off, her partner in tow.

Dave and Johnny Mack stayed to help while the father got his three children ready to go. The father would take them to their aunt's house, and then go to the hospital himself.

This wasn't a family that was well off. Although the apartment was large, it only had two bedrooms. One for the parents, one for the four children. There wasn't much furniture besides the couch and the TV. Dave wasn't the kind to point fingers at the choices people made. Everyone was different, with a story of their own.

The father came out of the bedroom with his three children, ready to go. There was an awkward moment when he and Dave locked eyes. The father turned his face away. Dave had seen that look before.

No matter how many times Dave went into people's houses, there was always that uncomfortable feeling. On the street, things were even. But all privacy was ripped away when the police came into a home. Everything showed. The embarrassed look of a person in their home was something Dave would never get used to.

As the father stood in his home, Dave could almost see what he was thinking. Was he a good provider? Were he and his wife good homemakers? Why didn't he and his wife clean up the mess? If they were good parents, how could such an accident happen? The pain of guilt had taken hold.

Dave and Johnny Mack turned to leave, but then Dave saw something he hadn't noticed: a little Christmas tree, up in a corner window.

The "tree" was a crooked, fake mini-pine, standing about a foot high on a window ledge. It had five, maybe six, decorations on it. But

26

it had lights that worked. A string of colored bulbs, about two feet in length, were wrapped around the tree, blinking on and off.

The two year old noticed where Dave was looking. He didn't understand his oldest sister was hurt, but he did understand the attraction of lights. He grabbed Dave's hand and led him to this, his most cheerful vision.

"Christmas tree," the little boy said.

"Yes," said Dave. "Beautiful."

The father came over to the child and policeman, and looked at Dave. There was no sarcasm in Dave's voice. The father picked the boy up, and straightened himself up.

"He loves that thing," the father said. "I had to put it up there so he don't run away with it."

"It is nice," replied Dave, patting the little boy on the back. Then he said to the father, "I know you're going to have your hands full now, I'll let you get going, sir."

The father nodded in appreciation, and started to put winter coats on his children.

* * * * *

Way before you became old enough to have people teach you otherwise, your mother's face was the most precious thing you'd ever seen. No singer or actress in the world could be prettier. And your father, was the biggest man in the world. Within his arms no harm could touch you. For all tiny children, these truths are gospel.

And if, during that same time in your life, before television showed you how to compare, and other kids taught you the meaning of shame, any little thing might be your source of pride and joy. An old teddy bear, a hand-me-down sweater, a pair of no-name sneakers. Or a crooked, one-foot Christmas tree with working lights to reflect off your wide-open, happy eyes. Your parents trying to bring a smile to your face, with the best they had.

Chapter Six

The Bell Rings

Dave and Johnny Mack walked out of an apartment building in Brooklyn. Their body temperatures were soaring from standing inside a hot apartment for about an hour. Neither flinched when the cold air rushed against them.

They got into their patrol car, and continued to roll around the precinct. Neither spoke for the better part of the next hour, and no sector car called for a sergeant.

The deejay on the radio couldn't decide if it was better to play Christmas songs or hits, so she alternated between the two. A chipmunk asking for a hula-hoop was followed by a group of boys telling everyone it was time to dance, because they were "back." During the holidays New Yorkers find the strangest things acceptable.

Dave broke the silence. "What do you think, Johnny, about that family?"

"Hard luck," Johnny Mack answered.

"Do you think they were bad parents?"

"We can't say that, Sarge. Not the cleanest apartment, but it wasn't like they were expecting company. Who knows what the story is, we can't know what's what in a couple of minutes."

"No, I've got four kids too, my house is always a mess." As Dave looked into the cold night, all the six-seven's streets seemed to blur. What he did see clearly was the immediate future for the parents of the little girl. "ACS is going to grill them."

Johnny Mack nodded his head in agreement. "That's for sure, Sarge. They'll look into everything. Their jobs, any drug-use, child abuse, how the kids do in school—everything."

"I couldn't make that call, if they used drugs or not. Nothing in the house as far as I could tell. They looked bad, but considering what happened, who wouldn't look a mess?" Dave said.

"It doesn't have to be drugs. Maybe they can't get good work. They might work long hours with low pay, maybe they're just trying to stay afloat," Johnny Mack rolled over a few thoughts in his mind. "The kids seemed to be fine; they weren't scared of their father."

One telltale sign of abused kids is the fear of their own parents. The little girl's brother and sisters didn't have apprehensive faces.

"No I didn't think there was abuse there…" The many possible scenarios of the family's situation passed through Dave's mind. "It was a just a case of very bad luck."

Dave had seen many tragedies over the years. Why some things have an affect on him and not others—who knew what went on in his head. Now Dave's heart told him that it was time to act. His own gut instinct was the most important voice he knew.

"I think I'm going to spend a few dollars to get that little girl something," Dave said. "They didn't look like they were going to have such a good Christmas, you know?"

"That would be nice," Johnny Mack said.

"But then, you can't give to one without getting for the others, can you? It'll be a little bit of money, but I think it'll be worth it—what's a couple of dollars?"

"It doesn't have to be all on you, Sarge," Johnny Mack said. "You saw Trish, she practically adopted the little girl right there in the apartment. We'll chip in, so will the boys in the precinct."

"Yes, the boys *can* chip in." Dave brightened up, as something he didn't quite understand started to form in his mind. Something that would affect him for precisely seven Christmases. Johnny Mack didn't know it at the time, but he had just rung a bell in Dave's head. A big one.

* * * * *

Out in the parking lot behind the precinct, three cops and a sergeant stood in a small circle. They were all in regular clothing as their shift was over, but the sergeant told them there was still work to be done.

"A few dollars, some small gifts," Dave said. "No big deal, we'll get everyone to chip in."

Trish and Kenny nodded their heads, but they looked towards Johnny Mack. The senior man had to make this decision. Johnny Mack was clearly with Dave on this one.

"We'll get the boys to help out a little," Johnny Mack said.

"How much do you think it would cost, Trish?" Dave asked. "To take care of that little group?"

Trish looked at Dave. "One hundred, one-fifty, should cover it."

"Okay then," Dave said as he thought out loud. "A buck a man— from a lot of men."

Dave looked each one in the eyes, and nodded. He got a nod back from each in turn. He knew that this contract was as good as any.

Chapter Seven

Dollar-up

"Vicky, we're going to do something about that little girl," Dave told me that night. When he told me the story, I knew his mind was made up. Of what, I wasn't sure.

"*We* Dave? Don't *we* have kids of our own?" I asked.

"Not you and me, Vicky—*us*, the precinct." Dave said. "We should do something about it. It's *our* precinct, and we take care of it. Plus, Johnny Mack and Trish say it'll be good for everyone to chip in."

* * * * *

The third platoon, also known as the four-by-twelve tour, formed in the muster room for roll call. Roll calls were for attendance, assignments, announcements. The cops got into a formation three deep, facing a podium in the front of the room.

"Attention to roll call," the sergeant called out from behind the podium. Every officer quieted down.

"Officer Martin."

"Here."

"Officer Carlton."

"Sarge."

"Martin, Carlton—sector Adam-Boy, twenty hundred [8:00 pm] meal."

"Officer Adams...."

* * * * *

The NYPD uses all kinds of code names and acronyms. When they target crime in one area, it might be called an "Operation Impact," or a "Take Back." The burglary specialists in the precinct are known as the "BAT Team"—Burglary Apprehension Team. The list goes on and on. Dave knew his Christmas effort needed a name. With cops, a good name was better than a good explanation. Luckily the name came naturally. The NYPD, a Christmas mission—it was simple enough.

The third platoon roll call formed up and faced front. The sergeant called out names and assignments. Afterwards the cops awaited further instruction, breaking news, or anything else worth listening to. On this night their sergeant didn't disappoint them.

"Okay everyone, got an important announcement for you," Dave said. "A little girl got burned real badly the other day, and it's up to us to do the right thing here." He paused a second to let it sink in. "It's time to make a difference. Blue Christmas, everyone—before you take your posts, dollar-up."

On cue, Johnny Mack and Trish walked to the muster room's exit. Dave joined them. No one got by without giving up a dollar.

* * * * *

Because he worked within the third platoon, handling the collection there was easy. The first and second platoons needed a little more work. The first platoon was the midnights, or late tour, while the second platoon was the eight-by-four, or day tour. Dave needed their dollars too.

Dave went after the first and second platoon supervisors first. After getting a dollar from them he asked them to spread the word that he was collecting. Johnny Mack and Trish started working the other platoons as well, one cop at a time. Since this movement had started on a four-by-twelve, the third platoon cops really got into the act.

While everything moved along at a good pace, Dave's eye caught a few glitches. Almost every cop gave up a dollar if a sergeant asked for one. Almost every one didn't ask why. Dave and his helpers asked a lot of cops, and got a lot of dollars. But Dave wasn't completely satisfied. Little bells were going off inside his head. "Almost" wasn't good enough.

Chapter Eight

Small Bumps

The C.O.'s monthly supervisors meeting: about twenty sergeants and lieutenants crammed into his office like sardines. McFadden saw it as a meeting of the minds. His staff saw it as a bore.

The C.O. didn't care if no one listened to him. He wanted it on the record that he had put out the information. Whenever a sergeant or lieutenant messed up, he dragged them back in his office and said that, "he told them so."

The X.O. of the six-seven was Captain Eugene Gentile. Gentile was the only one who listened to McFadden while he rambled on. His eyes and facial expressions showed his keen interest. His concentration was so intense that he never noticed that all the sergeants were mimicking him.

To Dave's surprise, his Christmas agenda came up as a topic in the C.O.'s meeting.

"You've got some sort of Christmas drive, going on Dave?" the C.O. asked.

"Yes sir, a Blue Christmas."

McFadden tapped his fingers on the desk as he repeated "Blue Christmas" a couple of times, measuring it against some of his past memories. Again the name won out over the explanation.

"Yes, yes, Dave," the C.O. said, "that's all well and good, this Blue Christmas thing you've got going on, but I'm getting robbery reports—does this ring a bell?"

The X.O. broke in, "are you talking about the three masked men robbing cabbies in the nineties, inspector?"

"No captain," the C.O. glanced sideways at Gentile. "I am referring to three of my uniformed staff, mugging *our very own officers,* in the hallways of our precinct." He looked around the room, "does anyone know about this?"

Gentile jerked his head back with an extra look of surprise. Every sergeant and lieutenant in the room jerked their heads back in a mock version of their X.O.. McFadden looked down for a second, and shook his head. Everyone in the room except Gentile knew he was trying not to laugh. The C.O. brought his head up with a serious face.

"Who will benefit from this Blue Christmas, Dave?" the C.O. asked.

"A little girl from the precinct, one of our aided-jobs. Her legs got burned pretty badly."

McFadden thought for a second, as he weighed the pros and cons. Years of experience had showed him many roads to hell.

"You've got to be careful, Dave," the C.O. said, "As policemen, anything to do with money can cause problems for us."

Lieutenant Randolph Jacobs, a big burly man, with scraggly gray hair and gigantic forearms chuckled, "Yeah, like that nit-wit Sardino, playing poker with Johnny Mack and the boys." He laughed out loud, but only a couple of supervisors dared to laugh with him.

The Sardino remark agitated McFadden, but he turned his attention back to Dave. "How much are you collecting from my officers?" he asked.

"One dollar, sir."

"That's it?"

McFadden calmed down, as all his doubts went back into their mental boxes. He then took out his own wallet, pulled out a dollar bill, and passed it down the line to Dave. Any Blue Christmas controversy was now settled.

When the dollar bill came into Jacob's hands, he looked at it and exclaimed, "Good lord, Dave, you've freed a prisoner—George Washington is blinking from the light!"

Jacobs threw back his head and let out a big, booming laugh. Now the C.O. was clearly angry. This time no one laughed with Jacobs.

* * * * *

It was two days before Christmas 1998. Dave, Trish and Johnny Mack were still going through the six-seven, dollar by dollar. Encouraged by momentum, Dave grabbed a dollar from anyone else he could. Cops from other precincts, EMT's, mailmen, deliverymen, all left the six-seven a dollar short.

By week's end they had over one hundred and seventy dollars. Dave was happy to tell me how smoothly things were going. But I couldn't imagine one hundred and seventy instances without some trouble.

"No one gave you a problem, Dave? I find it hard to believe that you didn't get *any* resistance."

He started to deny it, but then he scratched his head and said, "Yeah, this one girl *did* give me a problem. Officer Harbor. She couldn't believe I asked her for a dollar. Like it was some kind of a big deal. Then she tells me that she works hard for her money."

I didn't interrupt Dave when he got like this, it only made him worse.

Dave went on with his story.

"Can you imagine, Vicky? For a buck. She put her hands on her hips and started shaking her head back and forth like a bobble-head doll. Unreal."

Officer Lisa Harbor was pretty, young, and a bit of a complainer. Unlike Trish, she didn't handle patrol well. She had landed a truant position, and dealt with school kids Monday through Friday, with weekends off.

Now Dave was marching around the living room with his hands on his hips, and shaking his head from side to side. He exaggerated what Officer Harbor had done to him the day before.

"Well, it is *her* dollar," I reminded him.

"Yeah, so what? It's only a lousy buck. What if I wanted to buy myself a coffee? She couldn't buy me a coffee? I'd buy her a coffee."

"It wasn't for a coffee, Dave, it was for something good. You should have explained that."

"Yeah, well I don't have time to give everyone an explanation, I've got to get lots of dollars. I told her to keep her stupid dollar. If you can't trust your sergeant, then you can forget it. Why be a cop?"

"I know you're not going from, "not giving a sergeant a dollar" to, "why be a cop?" are you Dave?" I couldn't stop him from getting passionate, but I did try to point out when he was overboard.

"It's the principle, Vicky. Besides, she *doesn't* work hard for her money. Harbor is one of the *laziest* cops I've ever seen. All she does is read fashion magazines in those schools all day!"

He started to mumble some bad words under his breath, so I didn't say anything else. Dave's hardheaded. He was also the kind of guy that would do anything for anyone. He wasn't happy about being questioned over a dollar. To make things right in his head, he had dealt out her punishment. Harbor wouldn't get to be an elf.

* * * * *

After roll call Dave stopped Officer Hector Byrce by grabbing his shoulder. Hector turned and faced Dave. They stood at the exit of the muster room, about fifteen feet away from the front desk. Dave would test the will of a stubborn cop.

"Sarge, I'll see you when I got it. You know I'm good for it," Bryce said. He pushed the hand off his shoulder and flexed his neck muscles.

"A dollar? You've been telling me for three days that you'll see me. You're trying to avoid paying one dollar?"

"Maybe I don't like the way you're asking, Sarge. What is this—a shakedown?" Bryce shouted to raise attention. "Maybe I ought to call Internal Affairs. Oww! What was that?" Dave punched Bryce hard in his arm.

In some commands, Bryce would have gotten sympathy from his peers. Bosses weren't allowed to shake down their cops. But here in the six-seven, the cops were a little tougher. They didn't mind a little roughhousing. In this station house, it was just funny.

The third platoon gathered around to watch the spectacle. Bryce was known for being cheap, and now someone was calling him to task. If he wanted to fight with a sergeant over a dollar, that was on him. Threatening to call Internal Affairs didn't win him any support, either.

Bryce looked around and saw that all of the cops were laughing at what they considered a good show. Dave started to throw punches in the air at an imaginary opponent.

"Hey Sarge, what are you doing?" Bryce sounded nervous.

"I'm shadow boxing. To warm up. I can see you're a fighter." Dave started making head feints to make more of a show. The third platoon roared with approval.

"What, Sarge?"

"Don't deny it, you've got the eyes of a killer. But I'm willing to take my chances. After I warm up a little, we'll go out to the parking lot and settle this. Once and for all, like men."

Again Bryce looked around, but there was no escape. Officers cheered even louder as Dave threw punches in the air with great skill.

The commotion got the six-seven's C.O. out of his office. He was greeted by Lieutenant Jacob's loud laugh.

"Look at that little guy take on Bryce!" he said to the C.O., "he's got some fast hands. Ha-ha!"

"What's going on, Randy?" McFadden asked his lieutenant.

Jacobs slapped himself on the leg, as if his C.O. had just made a joke. "What, Dr. Frankenstein? You're asking me about *your* creation?" He pointed in the direction of Dave and Bryce and laughed again.

When the C.O. saw Dave shadow boxing and Johnny Mack leading the cheers, his hand went to his bald spot on the back of his head. He rubbed his scalp in thought for a second. He almost stepped forward to say something, but stopped. Instead he turned around and went back into his office.

"Here you go Sarge, I forgot, I have a dollar. Oww!" Dave hit Bryce in the arm again. "What was that for? I gave you the dollar."

"You got me all hyped me up, Hector—let's go in the back lot anyway!"

40

The cop shook his head and walked away quickly. He wanted no part of these kinds of games. Dave called after him, "Thank you for your support, Bryce-ster. Now a little girl won't be so blue."

Bryce called back from the exit door. "Yeah, great Sarge. I think these bumps on my arm are going to be blue—black and blue."

* * * * *

Officer Harbor started to hear stories and decided to get her dollar in. Through one of her friends. She got a senior cop, Vinny Vitale, to give in her dollar. She was too afraid to face Dave herself. I didn't blame her.

Vinny Vitale was a senior cop rumored to be an extra in the movie "Saturday Night Fever." His off-duty clothing revealed his love of the seventies. He worked out all the time, but still looked soft.

With all of his quirks, Vinny still had a reputation of being a super cop. He had been a rookie in the eighties, when crack cocaine wars spread violence throughout the city. Neighborhoods like the six-seven were hot spots. While most of these experienced cops went onto become detectives and bosses, Vinny stayed in the six-seven as a uniformed cop. His presence was appreciated by all.

"Hey Lee-sa," he said, "Why didn't you give the Sarge a dollar?"

"He didn't give me an explanation, Vinny."

"He's a sergeant, Lisa, and it's only a dollar."

"So?"

"So, if it was me, I know I wouldn't want that… a sergeant looking at everything I did or didn't do, because he was mad. I think you're in deep, Lee-sa. Over a dollar."

The thought of being scrutinized by an unhappy sergeant sank in. "Oh Vinny, what should I do?" She grabbed his hand and gave Vinny a wide-eyed, helpless look.

Vinny looked her in the eyes, but only for a second. He turned his head away and started to mumble.

"Well, uh, you know, for a damsel in distress…I'd fix things, Lisa."

"A *damsel*, Vinny? I am your princess, aren't I?"

Most men would believe that this was a pivotal moment. Any woman would know that Vinny was done as soon as he came over.

"Can you help me, Vinny?"

"Yeah, Lee-sa." Vinny threw out his chest, and combed back his hair. "Give me a dollar."

"Oh thank-you Vinny!"

She gave him a big hug and a peck on the cheek. Then she hit him with the smile. The kind that was saved for heroes.

Vinny took the dollar bill, and walked away like she gave him gold. He started to strut. Under a pair of tight uniform pants, his butt moved in rhythm to a Bee-Gee's song inside his head.

Nearby Rex and Adams watched with disgust.

"Would you look at that," Rex said to Adams, "that fool is going to rip his pants again." And then he called out to Vinny, "Hey Disco-Vin, you're blushing in public, man!"

Adams shook his finger at Lisa, who was smiling with girlish pride. "It's not nice to hypnotize our elders," he said.

In all cultures the younger learn from the older. Vinny had taught Lisa a good lesson. It had only cost a dollar, a kiss, and a smile.

Blue Christmas Lesson #1

There's nothing like a group effort.
Yes Vicky, let everyone be a *groupie*!

Chapter Nine

Great Expectations

By the afternoon of Christmas 1998, our kids were fully involved with their new toys. Every belly was full of turkey, gravy and cranberry sauce. It was easy to feel lazy, but Dave was ready for his four to twelve. And on this Christmas night, there was no problem going into work.

Dave had an important delivery to make. He had worked hard to gather a few dollars to buy presents for a burned little girl and her siblings. He was excited like a kid himself.

"Will Johnny Mack and Trish help you today?"

"My elves will be there, Vicky. Ready to go."

Over the past week Dave had begun calling Johnny Mack and Trish his "elves."

* * * * *

Trish had done the Christmas shopping. Her elfin job was to add a woman's touch to the Blue Christmas.

Johnny Mack picked himself a different job. He snooped around to find cops who hadn't donated to the cause. He found nothing more amusing than getting Dave riled up over a dollar.

"Sarge! Sarge! This one here—he didn't buck up!"

Dave would come running, fists in the air. "What? Where? Which guy, Johnny?"

Johnny Mack and the boys laughed as the mugging ensued. Dave knew the guys were making fun of him too, but at the same time it helped his cause. And he needed all the help he could get.

* * * * *

Dave took most of the money he had and gave it to Trish. She bought some toys and a few pieces of clothing for the injured girl and her siblings. She sat down by a table after the Christmas roll call so that everyone could see. Then she pulled out some wrapping paper, scissors, tape, and ribbons to make bows. All the policemen nodded as she worked. All in all, the Christmas drive had been a success.

Dave and Johnny Mack watched Trish with anxious faces.

"Don't worry," Trish said, "any child would be proud to get these gifts for Christmas. I went to the same place when I shopped for my nieces."

She looked up at the two, and washed away all their doubts with her winning smile.

Johnny Mack helped Dave get some teddy bears. He knew of a teddy bear factory located at a secluded corner within the six-seven. The six-seven had a few blocks in its southeast side that had factories and warehouses. The owner gave Dave two teddy bears at a wholesale price. He had told me about it on Christmas Eve.

"Vicky, I got some huuuge teddy bears! The real big ones."

"How big, Dave?"

"The big guys—that everyone tries to win at the amusement park?"

"The really big, big ones?"

"Yeah, remember that time we went to Great Adventures?"

"When you lost all those quarters, Dave?"

"Yes, that time, when the other guy won one. And his wife was yelling at him? Because he walked off with his big bear, but forgot his kid?"

"Yes Dave, I remember that."

"Well that's the kind, Vicky—where you spend every last quarter you own to get it, and then you forget your kid because of it."

Dave had never won a bear. But he had managed to get one for this little girl. He marched around pretending to carry the big bear. I could almost see the enormous teddy in his outstretched hands.

"The *Biggie Bear*, Vicky! And you know how we got them? Because everybody chipped in!"

* * * * *

The gifts were almost ready for the little girl. Dave watched over Trish nervously as she put the last touches on the gifts. He was too clumsy at things like wrapping. He didn't try to help, or even make a suggestion. She did her job nicely.

Except for the teddies, all of the presents were wrapped in decorative paper. The bears were adorned with big, red bows.

Dave had that confident, happy feeling of a job well done. Trish wasn't keen on going to the hospital, so Dave brought the gifts with Johnny Mack. It was all about doing the right thing.

On the way there, he imagined bringing in the gifts. They would be in uniform for the delivery. He imagined the smile that would come to the little girl's face. A pair of cops bringing her gifts… like Santa's elves.

* * * * *

Naive didn't begin to describe what Dave's thoughts had been. At the burn unit a nurse told them that the little girl was being scrubbed. She said that the two policemen should come back another time. Her tone was plain and simple.

The two cops looked at her and each other. Johnny Mack asked the nurse, "What are we supposed to do with these gifts?"

She shrugged her shoulders. "Bring them back on another day," she said. The two officers had never run into a burn unit nurse. This lady was tough.

Dave and Johnny told the nurse that they really didn't have the time to go and come back. They were here on their lunch hour. They didn't work anywhere near the hospital. Then they explained that they wanted to deliver the gifts personally. Could she help them, since this was Christmas night?

The nurse stopped for a moment to look at the two faces in front of her. She understood that they didn't understand. If it were that important, she would oblige.

She warned Dave and Johnny Mack that the little girl wouldn't be coherent. Because she was getting scrubbed. The nurse let this information sink in for a moment. The two still didn't comprehend.

"Scrubbed?" Dave asked.

The nurse explained that burn patients had to get their wounds scrubbed and cleaned so infections wouldn't get in. She nodded her head towards the patient rooms.

The two policemen looked in the direction she pointed. There was screaming coming from inside of one of the rooms.

Although the curtains were drawn at the window, the shadows

behind them told the story of a little girl's struggle. Two nurses held her down while the other one worked. She was getting *scrubbed.*

Dave looked at the nurse in front of him and she nodded her head, yes. As in yes indeed. That was the little girl that they had come to see.

* * * * *

When they left the hospital, Dave was feeling sick to his stomach. He actually thought that he could make this little girl happy by bringing her gifts. Gift-giving cops and smiles of appreciation. He realized that he had made up a fairy-tale in his head.

Because of the circumstances of the accident, the parents weren't allowed to see the child. ACS had lots of questions for them. And lots of restrictions, too.

The little girl was a patient in the hospital, and she was all alone. The only things that would help her were a sterile environment, medicine, love, and time.

For Dave, it was a cold dose of reality. The "big" gifts were small things in the little girl's world of pain. She had fallen into more than a hot bath. She had fallen into a state of circumstances far beyond the reach of Dave, or anyone else.

* * * * *

That night when Dave came home, I was excited and wanted to hear all about it. I asked him how his Christmas project went.

By the sad look on his face I thought Dave didn't get to see the girl. He just shook his head. I gave him a little time to get settled.

He told me about his visit after he took a shower.

"Vicky, it was bad. We put on sterile plastic suits over our uniforms. Masks and caps, too. For the germ-free environment. The cop-look was gone, we looked like astronauts."

Dave told me how the little girl lay shaking in pain on her bed. She was oblivious to everything, including him and Johnny being there. They tried to speak to her, but she was in too much pain. Her glossy eyes looked out into nowhere.

When I asked Dave about her parents, he told me that there was an investigation of neglect. The parents weren't allowed to see their child.

After a while, Dave said, "We didn't have close to what she needed."

I know he wanted to swoop down into that little girl's hospital room to make a difference. To spread a little happiness. But this one gesture, on this one day, was greatly overshadowed by her tragedy.

* * * * *

That night, by the light of our neon clock, I could see Dave staring out into the darkness as he lay in bed. It was a hard look in his eyes, as he kept his stare on something far away. Something painful, something he couldn't stop seeing in his mind's eye. He stayed this way for a long time before he finally went to sleep.

Blue Christmas Lesson #2
**You don't become the greatest person
in the world by trying to do the right thing.
Not by a long shot.**

Chapter Ten

Coffee Breaks

After a cold, hard winter, nothing brings back hope like spring. There wasn't much green in the six-seven, but the change in weather was enough to do the trick. The warm air felt like it was full of second chances.

There is always a top-cop in every precinct. This was a line that could be traced back throughout the years. Before the mischievous Johnny Mack, there was Angry Bob. Angry Bob went to work with the Detectives upstairs, who decided that "Angry" was unsophisticated, and therefore only referred to him as, "Big Bob." Some years back there was Prince Richard, the Tricky One.

The spring of 1999 had brought hope back to the six-seven indeed. Prince Richard had returned, and was now the king.

* * * * *

Richard Blackman had been a captain for six years. He should have been promoted to the rank of inspector long ago. But Blackman had a bad coffee allegation hanging over him.

In 1998 Blackman headed a new crime fighting initiative. There were mixed reviews on its success. The big chiefs called him to police headquarters to give a report on "Operation Tripod."

One high-ranking chief decided to show everyone that Tripod was a big flop. As Blackman tried to give his presentation, Chief Stokley interrupted him rudely, and often. The chief was not only a heckler that Blackman couldn't get rid of, but someone that he had to treat politely. It was a rough first half.

After a short coffee break, Blackman was about to continue with his presentation.

Blackman asked the chief's assistant, "Detective Henry, where's Chief Stokley?"

"Uh, he's in the bathroom, sir."

Blackman took a sip of his coffee. "Well I guess we should wait, I wouldn't want to continue without my greatest supporter. What do you think, Henry?"

"I'll check on him, captain."

Detective Henry came back shortly without Stokley and said that Blackman should go on without him.

"What's Stokley doing?" asked another, Chief Hart.

Henry walked over to the chief and whispered something.

"What! Someone spiked his coffee?"

"What's that, Hart?"

"Coffee?"

All the chiefs were asking questions at once.

"I don't know," said Chief Hart, "Stokley can't get himself out of the bathroom. Says the coffee's spiked with some sort of laxative."

A hush went through the room. One by one, all of the cups were placed on the big boardroom table.

Blackman finished his presentation smoothly. He made eye contact with everyone in the room, slowly sipping his cup of coffee. Each one in turn gave him a nod back, a few looked frightened. For the rest of the meeting, no one else offered criticism. Only Blackman drank the coffee.

* * * * *

Rumor had it that an angry big shot sent Blackman to the six-seven as a punishment. For Blackman, getting assigned to the six-seven as its new C.O., was nothing more than coming home.

In May of 1999 the new C.O. responded to the aftermath of a police shoot-out. Armed bandits robbing a grocery store, an observant bystander calling 911. The police showed up, and three robbers found themselves trapped.

The robbers tried to shoot their way out. After a brazen gun-battle they were captured. Bullets had found their way into the store's windows, cars on the street, a mailbox on the corner, and two of the perps.

Blackman and his X.O., Gentile, ran up to Dave, who had Rex on the ground with one leg in the air. Adams was sitting on Rex's stomach, pulling on his partner's pant leg.

"I got the leg, Nicky, push his pants down and let me see that knee."

"Got it Sarge."

"Get off me, I'm fine!" said Rex, struggling to get up.

Johnny Mack came over with his gun out. "What happened to Rex?"

"He says his knee—I gotta check it. Hold still Rex! He's going into shock Nicky, slap him."

52

Adams slapped his partner across the face.

"Wait," said Johnny Mack, "Rex wasn't in the shoot-out, he came afterwards."

Dave stopped and looked at Rex. "Why am I looking at your knee?"

"I fell getting out of the car," said Rex. "I just told you it hurt, I didn't say I got shot."

"We've just been in a shoot-out, don't come telling us about your boo-boo's," said Johnny Mack. "You two need to get over to that store and help set up the crime scene."

As Rex and Adams ran towards the store, Blackman and Gentile came up.

"What do you have, Dave?" Blackman asked.

"Robbers Capt, three sectors surrounded the store, Johnny and I backed them. All three perps shot at us, they're all captured, all my cops fired their weapons—I've got cops setting up the crime scene—we're all okay."

Normally a hyper guy, Dave was now a rocket ship. As he spoke to his C.O. he looked everywhere, ready to jump. As Rex had soon found out.

With a gun in one hand, and a full cup of coffee in the other, Dave's hands moved as fast as he spoke. Blackman didn't blink as Dave's gun whizzed by his head. He was a cop, guns were no problem. The coffee in Dave's other hand however, could be dangerous. Captains wore white shirts.

While keeping a careful eye on the cup of coffee, Blackman gently helped Dave put the gun back into his holster. The C.O. motioned for his X.O. and the boss of the detectives, Lieutenant Antonio Russo, to come over. He figured he could use a couple of extra hands to handle the coffee situation, but when he turned back around, Dave had already jumped back into the crime scene barking out about twenty different orders to his cops.

Blackman addressed his X.O. and Lieutenant Russo as they ran up.

"Did you see that?" Blackman asked.

"Yeah," said Russo, "Big problems if we don't fix that."

"What?" Gentile asked his C.O..

Russo jumped in. "Headlines!" he said, as he spread apart his hands like he was reading a billboard. "Cop gets into shoot-out without putting down his coffee."

"What? The news? Coffee?" the X.O. was flustered.

Blackman continued, "Think about it Gene. Dave's just been in a shoot-out, and he still has a full coffee in his hand. Reporters might say something terrible like he was taking little sips between shots—like a shootout wasn't important enough for the sergeant to put down his cup of coffee!"

Russo nodded his head in agreement, "Yeah, this could get bad."

Gentile's mind tried to digest the information. He tried to think about it logically.

"Okay… but what if Dave got the coffee *after* the shoot-out?"

Russo was puffing away on a cigarette. "When does he got time to grab a coffee, Capt? The only store around is shot to hell, ba-da-bing! You know what I'm saying?"

Russo pointed to the bullet-ridden store, and the X.O. agreed. No cup of coffee could have made it out of there. Dave had that coffee *before* the shootout. Russo crushed out his cigarette with his shoe and pulled out another.

"Even if he got that coffee *afterwards*, the news would pound us." Russo punched one hand into his other. "What kind of a guy gets into a shoot-out, and *then* gets himself a cup of coffee? Ma-lone! A cigarette you could understand, but *coffee?* Ba-da-bing!"

Blackman put his hands on Gentile's shoulder. "The Chiefs are going to be here any second. The press will come too. Gene, go get that cup of coffee out of Dave's hands before any Chiefs get here, or the press. Quickly, please."

"I see," said Gentile. But he didn't see or understand anything. Especially why he was in the six-seven.

Gentile looked around. Cops and squad cars were everywhere. So were ambulances and EMT's. Detectives of all kinds were showing up, scribbling notes in their memo-books. The high-ranking chiefs had also started to arrive, and they wanted to know everything—two minutes ago. Gentile's head started to spin as tried to anticipate the questions.

The six-seven was just too crazy for Gentile—he'd have to get a transfer out. As the X.O. stepped into the street he saw Dave whiz by, coffee still in hand. He moved forward with speed and determination. He had to get that coffee.

* * * * *

Dave stepped into the C.O.'s office. Blackman sat at one desk, Gentile at another.

"You wanted to see me, Capt?" Dave asked Blackman.

With a coffee in his hand, Dave gave a sideways glance at the X.O.

Gentile kept his head down as he looked over papers. After the coffee incident he interacted with Dave as little as possible. This amused Blackman to no end, especially since he had started it.

"Yes Dave, come in. You're the new training sergeant. The rookies come out of the academy next week and you've got them. Congratulations."

Most sergeants wanted nothing to do with rookie training. It required a lot of work and patience. When you were used to experienced cops, rookies were a downgrade.

The C.O. wanted his new officers trained well. Dave was unconventional, but he was enthusiastic. Blackman liked what he saw in his sergeant. It was also clear to him that Dave understood the secret.

Dave started to protest, but Blackman cut him off. "Look Dave, good training is important. That's how I began, right here in the six-seven. Let's get these rookies started off the right way."

"Me doing the training? I'm pretty new myself."

"You're more than capable. Besides, I heard you got that psycho, Johnny Mack, to help you with a Christmas drive. Is that true?"

"Yes, Capt, Johnny's good people."

"Well, if you can do that with a seasoned veteran, think of what you'll do with some fresh young minds. You could have yourself a bunch of new elves when you're done."

Dave knew he had no choice. He took another look at Gentile, who still hadn't said a word.

Blackman saw Dave wasn't quite finished. "You have anything else, Dave?"

"Yeah, Capt, I was just going to the store. Would you like me to bring back a cup of coffee?"

Before Blackman answered, Dave nodded towards the X.O., who still had his head in his paperwork. "Or maybe Captain Gentile wants to wrestle me for this one?"

Gentile looked up, ever perplexed. Dave held a cup of coffee in front of him, and shook it back and forth, just out of reach.

The X.O. couldn't believe a sergeant had that much nerve. No matter what had happened before. He stood up to say something, but couldn't get it out. He shook his finger at Dave and stuttered something that wasn't English. Dave made a funny face and walked out.

The X.O. fell short of making impact. He always did. Behind his desk, Blackman almost smiled.

Chapter Eleven

Rookie Adventures

At orientation Dave looked at his group of rookies with interest. "Did I ever look like that?" he wondered. They all looked so new. Their shields were shiny, their uniforms crisp. Their faces looked nothing like veterans of the streets.

People don't like the police because they only show up when there are problems. If everything's fine, you don't need the cops. But if you get into an accident, or someone steals your mailbox, or if your neighbor practices his trumpet by your window at three in the morning, then it's time to call the police.

Policemen know you don't want them around. And unless they're rookies, they're used to your disappointment when you see them. But— you say—you like the police. Really? When was the last time you were happy to see flashing lights in *your* rearview mirror?

* * * * *

Officer Enrique Villar, one of Dave's rookies stood in front of the desk with a prisoner. It was his first arrest and he was nervous. The Desk Officer looked at the rookie and his paperwork with disgust.

Dave, Johnny Mack and a couple of "rooks" watched from the muster room. Dave and Johnny Mack had told the rooks that they would teach them how to make arrests and do paperwork. Dealing with Desk Officers would be something that they would have to learn on their own. They all tried to peek their heads out from behind a wall to look.

"How's Ricky doing?" one of the rookies asked. At six-foot five, Trevor Yarde towered over everyone.

"The sergeant at the desk is chewing him up, all right," Johnny Mack answered.

"You're not a real cop until you have a nasty old Desk Officer yell at you," Dave told them.

"Sarge, did you get yelled at by Desk Officers when you were a rookie?" Trevor asked.

Dave smiled as he thought back to his own rookie days.

* * * * *

At the center of any precinct there's a wooden desk built from the floor up. It's about the size of small house. NYPD tradition states that the Desk Officer runs the station house from this structure.

Those who approach the desk find themselves up against a giant wooden wall, with something worse behind it. The Desk Officer sits high at the desk and looks down on all who come before him. Angrily.

Because a long time ago, there was a nasty old Desk Officer who scowled at everyone. Running a station house was an important task, and those who interrupted him would suffer his wrath. Soon word spread about this Desk Officer. Go near him, and he would rip your head off.

Other Desk Officers across the city took note. They realized their brother was right: the crabbier they were, the less they were bothered. All the Desk Officers banned together and took a solemn oath: to be grouchy at all times. Inside their precincts they terrorized anyone who came near them. Back at their homes they threw forks at their wives and children.

* * * * *

Dave, the rookie transit cop, stood in front of the midnight Desk Officer, with a prisoner in handcuffs. Sergeant Taylor was in his late-forties, had salt and pepper hair with a thick moustache, and was working on his potbelly.

Taylor sat puffing away on a cigar that was clearly against the department's smoking policy. He had done his time on patrol, both as a cop and a sergeant. Now in the twilight of his career, he resigned himself to the fact that he would roam no more. Like a once great lion of the plains, age had slowed him down. It was as if the hunters had caught the older beast, and threw him into a cage. The only moving he did now was behind his huge desk. During the hours of midnight to eight in the morning he paced back and forth behind it and growled at anyone who came near.

Along with his prisoner, Dave had a shopping cart full of junk, and something that looked like an old-fashion radio with a round screen. The Desk Officer shook his head in disbelief while Dave tried to explain to him what an oscilloscope was.

"A complainant, officer, do you have a *complainant*?"

Desk Officers hated anything out of the regular routine, and this rookie was ruining his night. Taylor hated rookies. Soon he would hate oscilloscopes as well.

"I'll get a complainant eventually, Sarge, but right now it's three in the morning—no business is open. I'll get to the bottom of it. You're not telling me to let this guy go when he's holding a thousand dollars worth of stolen electronics, are you?"

Taylor knew the rookie was right. Dave's junk collector had a brand-new piece of sophisticated electronics. The man had no explanation of how or where he got it. And like the Desk Officer, he had no idea what an oscilloscope was.

The prisoner would be charged with stolen property, but who owned it? A prosecutor would need a *complainant*—someone to say the oscilloscope was theirs.

Arrests like this clogged up the system. The prosecutor wouldn't write a complaint without a complainant. He would ask the officer to go find the person to press charges. Finding an owner wouldn't be easy; an oscilloscope wasn't like a car. Cars were registered. Finding the owner of electronic equipment could prove futile.

The Desk Officer stared at Dave. If he were in a cartoon smoke would be coming out of his ears.

* * * * *

Dave's rookies spent the summer and fall months learning to become good cops. On a cold fall day they filled a police van. As Johnny Mack drove, everyone looked around and geared up to run. Bootlaces were tied tight and double-knotted. Rubber bands were placed around their keys, and hats were placed out of the way.

Johnny Mack slammed on the brakes. In front of a building a cloud of marijuana smoke filled the air. A group of thugs froze at the sight of the police, but only for a second. The van doors flew open. Ricky and Trevor jumped out first. The chase was on.

Chapter Twelve

Going Postal

As Christmas of 1999 approached, Dave, Trish and Johnny Mack had to make a choice. They decided that there was no reason to break the momentum. If anything, they could take it up a notch. So for the last Christmas of the millennium the trio decided to take two dollars from everyone.

"What are you up to for this year's Christmas, Dave?" I asked him.

"Well I've got no specific cause this year, Vicky. I'm going to collect some Santa letters at the post office. I've heard about good stories on the news, so I figure we'll join in. You know, why not?"

Blue Christmas Lesson #3
Don't ask "why not?"
Because you'll soon find out.

Dave left the borough of Brooklyn and went to the largest post office in New York City. It was in Manhattan on 8th Avenue, from 31st all the way to 33rd street. He found out the Christmas letters were unlike anything he expected.

Each year at Christmas time the post office takes letters to Santa and puts them on giant tables. The public is welcome to come and look through them. Dave walked in and joined dozens of possible Santas.

For Dave looking through the hundreds of letters was like rummaging through a weird lottery. The idea was nice enough. Kids writing letters to Santa, the letters placed on display. There were big tables, with plenty of people looking through them.

* * * * *

"So how many letters did you get?" I asked him when he came home that night.

"Not that many, maybe about fifty. It's a strange thing going through those letters at the post office."

"How's that, Dave?"

Dave had spent about three hours going through the letters, and the experience had drained him.

A lot of kids—and parents too—were precise about what Santa should bring them. For instance, if they asked for clothes, they were explicit about the brand. For the first time in his life Dave became familiar with designer labels. He didn't know Santa was supposed to have style.

He found out that jewelry would be a nice gift from Santa. Electronics were also a popular choice. Televisions, stereos, lap top computers, x-boxes were all remedies to cure the Christmas blues.

Dave was collecting two dollars from everyone he could in the six-seven this year, but it was still a small operation.

"Vicky, we couldn't afford some of the stuff they're asking for."

I put a Spanish coffee with hot milk in front of him to pick up his spirits. He fiddled with the spoon and breathed in the aroma. He smiled and stretched. Sometimes my husband needed simple pampering.

"I don't know Vicky, I was just looking to help out some kids. With little things, you know?"

"Maybe all the good letters were taken. How many did you go through?"

"Tons, Vicky. Tons and tons. Everybody's writing to Santa. Schoolteachers get into the act, too. Whole classes write letters to Santa. Unless the kids need it, why throw those letters in the mailbox? It competes with the kids who don't have."

"Hmmm."

"And you know another problem?"

"What's that?"

"I'm not sure who's really needy, I just can't tell."

"What do you mean Dave?"

"I mean every kid wants something, but there's no way of knowing who's who. How can you tell if a kid is needy just by reading a letter?"

"I see."

"But more than that, you've got your moms writing in—and they're all *crazy*."

Dave read through some letters that mothers had written and couldn't believe them. They were nothing like the letters to Santa that the kids wrote.

Some mothers asked for clothes, not only for their children, but for themselves as well. They carefully wrote out the sizes and brands they wanted. Dave found out that Nike actually made a "baby Jordan."

A lot of moms asked for jewelry. Some bluntly asked for cash. Help with the rent. Or something for their man, who was away. Because the police wrongfully locked him up. This offended Dave. Because if a guy was wrongfully in jail, then they should say that a prosecutor wrongfully prosecuted him. And a jury wrongly convicted him. And a judge wrongfully sentenced him.

As Dave read through more of the mom letters, he got the feeling some thought they were writing to a dating service. Personal information like their good looks and pet names were in some letters. And how they had no boyfriend.

"I don't know if they were looking for presents or trying to find a new daddy," Dave said.

In the end, Dave didn't pick one letter written by a mother. None were humble enough. He wasn't about to participate in their "Christmas lotto."

Fifty letters from his postal adventure would do.

* * * * *

Dave went back to the teddy bear factory to get some bears at a good price. The eccentric Steven Smith greeted him at his desk.

Steve Smith was a fifty-year old man, with glasses and curly dirty blond hair. Like his teddy bears, he didn't have one mean bone in his body. Unlike his bears, he never stopped moving. He built his business from a pushcart into a factory.

Every time Dave went into Steven's place he had to get out of the way, or get run over. Workers went by in a hurry, carrying loads of papers, boxes, and bears. In a huge open room workers sat talking on phones and writing down orders. Through a pair of giant double doors were endless rows of shelves filled with bears in boxes. Behind the shelves the bear makers with their sewing machines, tried to catch up to the orders coming in. Dave thought to himself that this had to be what the North Pole looked like.

The "desk" that Steven worked in front of was an ever-growing monster. It had started as a desk against a wall. Then a hutch was added on. Over the years an additional desk was added to each side. Shelves were built on these. Every drawer and shelf was overflowing with files, catalogues, papers. The corners of the files and papers looked like the jagged scales of a dragon.

Finally a round lunch table was put opposite the monster desk. Smith put two phones on this lunch table and did his work from there. Little paper dragon piles were already growing by his phones, threatening passerbys with paper cuts.

As Dave stood by to order teddy bears, he was amazed to see Steven work. The man spoke on both phones and at least three factory workers at the same time. He took Dave's order and dispatched it pronto.

"Move on this order quickly! For the love of God, can't you see that this man will put me in handcuffs!"

"C'mon Steve, you know I'm happy you're helping me," Dave said.

"Just go with this, Dave," Steve whispered, "I don't get to have fun." He looked around the room and said, "I work in a teddy-bear factory, you know?" Steve started yelling again, "Quickly with those bears! He's going to give all of your cars tickets! He needs to be out of here in the next five minutes!"

* * * * *

Dave's rooks became good at police work. They were well trained, and had already become known as capable officers. But for Christmas, their sergeant told them that they were going to be elves. Some of the senior cops were going to be elves too, so they didn't question the matter. Besides that, they knew that questioning their sergeant caused him to start punching.

Christmas was shaping up the way Blackman had said it would. Dave had a small army of elves, all ready to go.

Chapter Thirteen

The New Elves Deliver

The Christmas drive at the six-seven had gone from one dollar to two dollars. In police talk, that's going from a cup of coffee, to a cup of coffee *and* a doughnut.

Blue Christmas was now a legitimate delivery route, with fifty stops. Dave's rookies helped deliver presents on Christmas Eve and Christmas Day of 1999. The couple of days off were well deserved after seven months of hard on the job training.

* * * * *

Armed with letters and presents, the elves started to deliver.

From the mouths of babes...

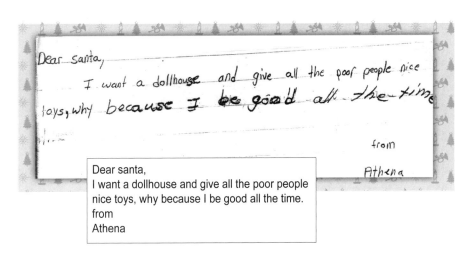

Dear santa,
I want a dollhouse and give all the poor people nice toys, why because I be good all the time.
from
Athena

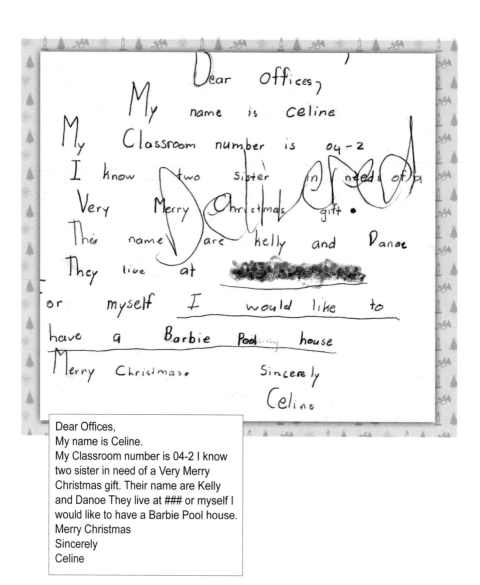

Dear Offices,
My name is Celine.
My Classroom number is 04-2 I know
two sister in need of a Very Merry
Christmas gift. Their name are Kelly
and Danoe They live at ### or myself I
would like to have a Barbie Pool house.
Merry Christmas
Sincerely
Celine

Dear Santa Claus,

My Name is Kevin, I am six Years old. I want a blue Power Ranger toy for christmas. I have two sisters. Their names are: Shymeeka (she's 7) and Talisha (she's 6) My brothers are 5 and a teen ager. I do not have a christmas tree.

Do you have an extra one?

Love,
Kevin

Dear Santa Claus,
My name is Kevin. I am six years old.
I want a blue Power Ranger toy for
Christmas. I have two sisters. Their
names are: Shymeeka (she's 7) and
Talisha (she's 6) My brothers are
5 and a teen ager. I do not have a
Christmas tree.
Do you have an extra one?
Love,
Kevin

Although most of the deliveries went off without a hitch, Dave wasn't satisfied.

"You know what bothers me, Vicky?"

"I'm sure I'm going to find out."

"You know we delivered all around Brooklyn today, and we must have hit about eight other precincts besides the six-seven."

"You couldn't get letters from the six-seven kids?"

"I did the best I could at the post office, but we only did about ten deliveries in our own precinct. There are plenty of kids in the six-seven that could use a visit."

"Hmmm."

"That's not all. A lot of the families had presents already. Only a few families really needed our visit."

"That still counts, Dave. Any real help does."

"Yes Vicky, but all that time and effort could have gone to better use. We want to reach out to the right families. We could have given out the gifts better."

"That's a shame, Dave. But what can you do?"

"That's the question, Vicky. What am I going to do?"

*****

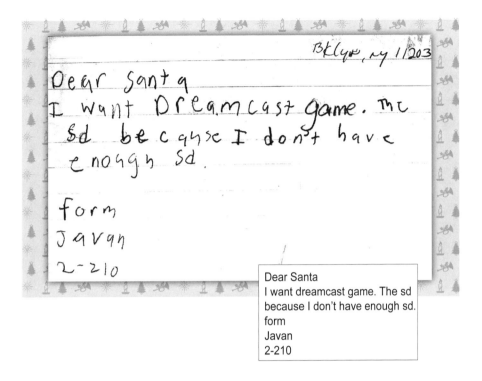

Dear Santa
I want dreamcast game. The sd
because I don't have enough sd.
form
Javan
2-210

A few cops stood outside a temporary shelter in Bushwick, Brooklyn. Families that lived in this building were on a waiting list to be placed into a permanent residence. Dave, Johnny Mack, Ricky and Trevor knocked and waited.

They knocked once. Twice. A few times more. A television and voices could be heard inside, but no one came to the door.

"It's a shelter, Sarge," said Trevor in his strong West Indian accent. "They probably need the gifts."

"Let's wait some more, Sarge," agreed Ricky.

Dave looked at the letter, and at the faces of his elves. He knew they were right. But Dave wasn't a patient man. He went and got the building's security guard.

"Yes, they're home," said the guard.

"But they don't answer," said Dave.

The guard looked at the policemen with their big bag, and then at the closed door. He took out a huge flashlight and started banging on the door. He muttered something about the first time the police doing a good job, and this is what they get. Then he started to yell as loud as he knocked.

The door finally opened. A lady stuck her head out. She wore a bathrobe and thin slippers. Her hair was half in braids and half in berets. She looked to be about forty.

"What do you want, Fitch?"

"Not me, them. The police want you."

"I didn't call. And I didn't do nothing wrong." She looked at the policemen. "Go 'way," she said.

She started to close the door, but Fitch stopped her. "Wait woman, these officers have something for your children."

A girl came to the door and stuck her head through. At the age of seven she was the oldest of her siblings. They stood behind her, trying to peak their heads through.

"Hi police." The little girl said.

"Hello little lady," Trevor replied.

Trevor took over the show. He took out the letter that she had written to Santa. He explained that sometimes Santa used different helpers, and on this occasion, it was the police. Then Trevor handed out the presents.

The girl smiled and started to thank the policemen. But a look from her mother made the girl stop talking and go back into the apartment. The mother tried to close the door again. Fitch put his hand out one more time. He felt obligated to the police. It might have been the first time in his life that he felt this way.

"Tara, you could be a little polite here." She stood stone-faced.

Dave saw something in her eyes that he had learned a year before. Small tokens from strangers would not change this lady's situation in life. He tapped the guard on the shoulder and gave him a nod to show it was okay.

Not satisfied, Fitch asked Tara one more question, "Why didn't you open the door before?"

"Because I didn't recognize the voices." This time she got the door closed.

Fitch's mouth dropped. To get the last word in he yelled through the closed door, "Well Tara, if this place catches on fire, you're not going to recognize the voices of the firemen trying to rescue you, and you will just burn woman! Burn!"

Fitch looked at the officers and didn't know what to say.

"Don't worry about it Fitch," Trevor said as he put one of his huge arms around the guard, "it's for the kids."

Blue Christmas Lesson #4

**But, it's for the kids. What are the "buts?"
There aren't any. It's for the kids, and don't
you worry about nothing else.**

Dear Santa Claus,

My name is M___
I am 7 years old, I have
Two brothers, S___ is 3 and
S___ is 5, My sister A___
is 6.
I would like a doll, I
think my brothers would
like a football and base ball
A___ also likes dolls.

How do you Fly with deers
in the sky?

Love
M___

Dear Santa Claus,
My name is M___. I am 7 years old.
I have Two brothers. S___ is 3 and
S___ is 5, my sister, R___ is 6.
I would like a doll, I think my brothers
would like a football and base balls.
R___ also likes dolls.
How do you Fly with deers in the sky?
Love
M___

Chapter Fourteen

Special Delivery

When you know someone well, they just can't hide things from you. That's why I've always wanted to play poker with Dave. So I could take all his money.

The lady at the shelter had him irritated. He had to get that story out. But more than that, he had to get it out of the way. I knew he had another story for me. His eyes were sparkling.

"So what else happened, Dave? Tell me what was good."

"Well there was one delivery that was *great*, Vicky, let me tell you."

I sat and watched the man I knew so well. Before my eyes he changed into an excited little kid. In the middle of the day he received a call. He didn't know it, but he had been waiting for this call for a year.

The father of the little girl who was burned called the precinct. Dave had been running in and out all day on deliveries. It was a miracle that he actually caught Dave in the precinct.

"Hello, officer?"

"Yes sir."

"I don't think you remember me, but you will remember my daughter. She was the girl whose legs got burned last year. You and your precinct brought presents to her at the hospital last Christmas."

The father told Dave that his daughter was now living at her grandmother's house. Dave asked about her legs. The father stated that physically, she was doing fine. Being a cop, Dave also asked about their living situation.

The father said that it would be a long process, but they were working on it. He and his wife were ready to take their children back. All their dealings with ACS were ongoing. There was a lawsuit on the building. But more than legalities, on this day he had called to ask for two police officers, and one favor.

Dave and Johnny Mack were only too happy to make that visit.

* * * * *

Curious to see the little girl, all the rookies piled into the van with Dave and Johnny Mack. This story had the makings of a six-seven legend and none of them wanted to miss it. Trish also climbed in for the visit. Johnny Mack seemed normal enough, but they had never seen their boss in this kind of mood before. Dave looked nervous, and although they weren't sure, giddy? The ride in the police van seemed smooth enough, but it sure looked like Dave's seat was going over a few bumps.

The grandmother's house was everything it should be. A nice, small, cozy home. Shiny decorations for Christmas were everywhere, but everything still looked neat. Grandma had on little glasses, over rosy cheeks and a big smile. All of the cops got cookies when they came in.

The little girl stood up as Dave, Johnny and Trish gave her a Christmas present. She looked healthy and happy. She wore white stockings that looked normal to everyone except for those who knew her situation. Dave looked questioningly at her grandmother.

"She'll be fine sergeant. As long as she takes her medicine and wears these stockings. As you can see she's strong and fit."

"And everything will be normal?" Dave asked.

"She will be one hundred percent fine. One hundred per-cent!"

Dave looked the girl over and couldn't believe his eyes. The last time he saw her she was all alone in a hospital bed, and couldn't respond to them. He and Johnny had to wear those white plastic suits, and they looked like astronauts. Now she was living happily with her Granny, and the Christmas tree was full of presents.

Dave looked around. By the pictures he could see the little girl's mother had grown up in this house. A pretty kid. A child with promise. Pictures showed her singing, receiving certificates, smiling for the camera. He remembered what her mother looked like in their apartment the year before. Life didn't come with guarantees. Granny's daughter had been through some hard times. There were more to come. In the meantime Granny was taking care of one of her granddaughters.

Dave turned his attention back to the little girl. She was shy, but she looked healthy. All the policemen in her grandmother's house made her curious. She started to run around a little, which made Dave nervous.

The grandmother laughed. "Don't worry Sarge, look." She made the little girl come to her. Then she pulled the stockings down a bit to show that her legs were fine.

She explained that the year had been hard. There were the endless wrappings and unwrappings of the legs. There was medication and therapy. There were at-home tutors. Dave, Trish and Johnny Mack nodded their heads as they took in granny's account.

The rooks politely stayed just outside the conversation. But their interest bordered on fascination. They knew Dave, Trish, and Johnny Mack as take-charge cops. As far as the rookies were concerned, whatever these veterans said, *went*. Now their mentors almost looked like children themselves, hanging on to an old lady's every word; and attentive to any little movement that a little girl might make.

The grandmother then pointed at Dave and Johnny Mack, and spoke to her granddaughter.

"These two came to the hospital last Christmas, to visit you. Do you remember them?" her grandmother asked.

The little girl shook her head, no. If there were white plastic suits around, Dave and Johnny would have thrown them on in a second.

"They brought you presents last year, girl."

"They did?" The girl smiled shyly.

"Yes. Don't you remember? They brought you your big bears?"

"My big, big bears, Granny?"

"Yes." Granny turned to Dave and Johnny and said, "She loves those two big bears, officers."

The little girl came up to Dave smiling. She tapped him on his hand. "Thank you, Mr. Police."

I asked Dave what he did. If he kept it professional, because his rookies were around. But even before he said it, I knew exactly what he did. After all, he was a father too.

"I waited a year for this," Dave said. "I picked her up and hugged that little girl!"

A few rookies now understood their sergeant as a man.

Blue Christmas Lesson #5
Some will remember.

Chapter Fifteen

A New Team

Dave's life had transformed into a Christmassy whirlwind for the last two years right around the holiday season, but police-work was his real bread and butter. Dave also knew that the liberties he got for his Christmas antics were directly related to how good of a job he did during the rest of the year. When holiday was over, it was time to get back to work. Besides, his career goal was to make it into an investigative squad to work with detectives. Maybe even to hold the rank of Detective Lieutenant, like his childhood hero, Colombo.

*****

Sector cars zip around their commands answering radio runs. But precincts also have specialty teams. Summons teams address traffic issues and write lots of tickets. Plain-clothes teams concentrate on violent crimes. Narcotic teams work on drugs in the streets. A conditions team — that would be team-catchall.

The conditions team worked on quality of life issues, or whatever the precinct's C.O. felt was important. Captain Blackman felt that his conditions team should clean up the rift-raft in the precinct. Their new sergeant felt the same way.

*****

After close to a year of training the rookie class, Dave started his new job as the conditions sergeant. Most of his rookies got assigned to the different platoons of the six-seven. But a couple of them got to work with him on the conditions team.

There was Trevor Yarde, the tall officer born in Jamaica, with a charming smile and booming laugh. He made people feel like he was the host of the six-seven because he greeted everyone so warmly. Even when he put perps in the police car he waved his hands like it was a limousine.

Officer Enrique Villar made it onto the conditions team as well. He had grown up in one of the rougher housing developments in South Queens. As a teenager, he stayed out of trouble by noticing everything. He knew that little things added up to become big things. It was as if his sharp eyes saw things before they happened. The team called him "Ricky Radar."

Brian Johnson was the team's speedster. He loved to run, and his fast legs came in handy. Everyone called him "Chase."

Johnny Mack liked working with Dave, so he joined the team as well. The new team was an immediate success. They went through the precinct's rift-raft like a vacuum cleaner.

✶✶✶✶✶

Not everyone was happy with the new team's success. Dave and his guys interrupted the "flow" of the midnight platoon.

Every midnight Desk Officer had to contend with a hectic first couple hours. A busy four-to-twelve shift would carry a lot of work over into the midnight tour. After a hectic beginning, the station house eventually calmed down around two or three in the morning, especially for the Desk Officer. The midnights enjoyed this "quiet time."

The conditions team marched in six prisoners via a late night operation. Every couple of weeks they changed up their hours to catch familiar targets, at unfamiliar times. The precinct had come to know this as the "midnight romp." The midnight platoon knew this as an attack on their quiet time.

Dave brought a bunch of forms with prisoner information behind the desk. He also had bags of vouchered property with him. As a sergeant he had to log these items into the command log. It was two-thirty in the morning, and the midnight platoon was twenty minutes into their quiet time.

The Desk Officer's assistant, the property officer, the telephone switchboard operator, and the prisoner-cell attendant all looked up with resentment. Another sergeant, sitting by the desk with paperwork, also looked up with disdain.

All eyes looked to the Desk Officer, Benjamin Scott. He had to do something.

"For Christ-sakes you moron, what are you doing to my book?" The midnight cops nodded their approval as Desk Officer Scott addressed the invader.

Dave was many years junior to Scott. "Gee Ben, I thought you were done with your entries. I'm sorry."

"The midnight desk is a complicated system, Dave, and dummies like yourself are forever messing up my book without asking permission."

Desk Officers were known to be overly protective of their command logs. It was the official record book of the precinct.

The conditions team knew Dave's facial expressions out on the street. When he got a certain look on his face, it meant they had to get ready to move. Because someone was about to get handcuffed. Dave's face had that same look, but now it was for his fellow sergeant. Here in the precinct, Dave's team had no idea what was going to happen.

The jaw muscles on one side of Dave's face clenched and his eyes narrowed. But Dave also knew he was a visitor on this platoon. He bit his tongue.

"Ben. I have some vouchers here. May I put them in the command log?"

"You know, I don't like your antics, Dave. I don't like your team, I don't like the perps you bring in, and I don't like *you* writing entries in *my* command log."

Inside Dave's head the bell rang.

"Then you should see what we leave behind," Dave said, now grinning with all of his teeth.

"What?" Benjamin asked.

Dave came closer to him as he spoke, and the senior sergeant wasn't quite sure what to do.

"Oh yeah, Ben," continued Dave. "We let all kinds get away. But we shouldn't do that, because the Law is the Law. And who am I, just a rookie sergeant. Deciding not to drag in all those law-breakers?"

"What are you talking about, Dave?"

"I'm talking about the next time we go into a crack house, we drag every last body in here. No discretion. Three druggies, four druggies, fourteen—one leg, crutches, wheelchairs—they all come in. Believe me, Ben, we can get into a lot of crack-houses."

Benjamin didn't like what his junior sergeant was getting at. Worse than that, he believed him to be capable of what he threatened.

Dave went on, "and what about jay-walking, Ben? Because traffic violations count, too. I'll stand outside the methadone clinic and run every jaywalker for warrants. Drag them in, too." Heroin addicts enrolled in methadone programs were notorious for moving slowly, and even falling asleep as they stood.

"Ben, you're showing me a new light! I believe I should thank—"

"Now don't get carried away, Dave! Here, give me those vouchers and prisoner forms. I'll put them in the log myself. I got a system, that's all I'm saying. Let me do things my way, I am the Desk Officer, aren't I?"

As Dave let Benjamin take over, the other midnight sergeant, Matthew France, had witnessed the exchange. He went to Scott and offered to speak to Dave. About respect, and seniority.

"No Matty! Don't get that guy upset, you have no idea what he'll do! Didn't you see that smile on his face?" Benjamin asked.

"Yeah, I saw him smiling," said the second sergeant.

"Well that ain't no smile," Benjamin said, "that's retardation. Did you see that look in his eyes?"

"Yeah, the lights were on Ben, but no one was home."

"There's bells ringing in that empty head. I'm talking about keeping my command log in order, and he's talking about filling my cells with junkies. He's been hit too many times, he don't think right."

Benjamin pointed his finger at his head, and made a couple of circles.

The other midnight sergeant nodded his head; his wobbling double chins emphasized his agreement. "Yeah Ben, he's hearing bells."

"Yeah, and you know what it's like outside the methadone clinic," said Benjamin. "They can't walk, those guys. They got bad bones from those drugs. None of them can make it across the street on one light. Dave's team would catch them all."

The two commiserated in their disgust. Benjamin continued, "jaywalkers from there? Our whole tour will be sitting on hospitalized prisoners. It'll cripple the platoon."

"Yeah Ben, boxing ain't good for the head."

* * * * *

Chase stood next to Dave as the two midnight sergeants conversed. "Hey Sarge," he whispered, "Do the other bosses always talk about you like you're not here? I mean we're not more than ten feet away from them. They have to see you're *right here*."

"Believe it or not, I'm used to it." Dave answered. "We're going to fix them though."

"How so, Sarge?"

Dave pulled out a twenty-dollar bill and gave it to Chase. "Go get a bunch of doughnuts and a big jug of coffee for the midnight guys. After all, we're guests on this tour. Make sure you get a bunch of the big creamy ones."

"Yes sir."

The rest of the night went on smoothly as the Desk Officer and his cohorts happily munched away on their snacks. Powdered sugar was everywhere. Benjamin even took Dave under his wing for a few minutes to show him how he logged his entries into his book. Dave nodded his head and listened attentively.

Chapter Sixteen

Out of the Blue

You don't make it through a number of years without facing problems. Everyday work shows who you are, but a real problem can define you. How you handle these problems is what makes or breaks your reputation, and your police career.

A local drug dealer, nick-named Scar Face, was terrorizing the precinct.

The C.O. and few of his staff sat in a town hall meeting. Blackman sat at a table with Lieutenant Russo on one side, and his community affairs cop, Seda Hutchinson, on the other. Dave sat beside Russo. The hall was packed.

One by one, people from the neighborhood got up to the microphone and expressed their fears.

"Captain, you must do something."

"Scar Face has besieged us."

"You have to protect our children, captain."

As others continued, Scar Face was blamed for more and more.

Seda Hutchinson got up and called for silence.

"Don't worry, you must know we are here to help!" He pointed at Dave. "This sergeant and his team will work especially on your problem."

There was silence for a few seconds. Seda was a fellow West Indian and well respected.

Blackman leaned over to Dave, "you see what these people are going through? You lock this Scar Face up and you'll bring these people peace of mind."

A doubter expressed out loud what many were thinking, "What is this one man, or this one team, going to do?"

A few more asked the same.

"How?" Seda shouted to the group. "He has done many good things—he has worked some magic in this precinct. Now he's working for you."

The crowd seemed satisfied.

Russo turned to Dave and said, "Okay magic-man, it's your show now—you'd better pull something out of that hat. Ba-da-bing!"

* * * * *

Scar Face was a short, squat man with a nasty disposition. He had moved into the neighborhood quickly and violently. The corners Scar Face and his cronies claimed became shooting zones. Rival dealers had become nothing more than moving targets.

Legend had it that Scar Face got the nasty scar on his left cheek in a foreign prison. He would brag to anyone that they couldn't handle prison the way he did. Although it did nothing for his looks, he wore his scar like a badge of honor. Fear was his only friend.

* * * * *

Dave and his team mapped out a plan along with stages. Stage one was to break down the myth that Scar Face was untouchable. The conditions team had to show the neighborhood that not everyone was afraid of Scar Face. Least of all, them. So they visited him on a daily basis. And they kept it friendly, to show they weren't scared.

Ricky Radar, who loved to chat, jumped in the middle of Scar Face and his cronies on the street corner.

"Scar Face, how about that scar? It's hideous, can't we get that fixed?"

Scar Face didn't smile. Neither did his men.

"What kind of doctors do they have in Trinidad?" Ricky asked.

Scar Face scowled, "Mi ano Trini, bobby-lon. Mi a Yardy." (I'm not from Trinidad officer, I'm Jamaican.)

"Yeah, yeah," continued Ricky, "I've got family in Guyana too. You know them. Remember my Auntie Gwennie? She used to feed you when you were young."

"Stop tel' lie, bobby-lon."

There was a nastiness in Scar Face's eyes that only comes from doing terrible things. As he looked at Ricky his hands clenched and his teeth grinded. But Ricky wasn't backing down.

Ricky Radar ignored Scar Face and spoke directly to the small crowd on the corner.

"It's true, just ask my Auntie. They found him in a shoebox. And that scar on his face was from a bad tricycle accident, when he was ten years old. Tell 'em, Scar Face."

Ricky Radar continued talking to the group as Scar Face's eyes reddened and his lips tightened.

"Did you guys know that me and Scar Face are cousins? My Auntie

Gwennie's fourth cousin and Scar Face's stepsister were pregnant in Haiti. She had a miscarriage, but it still makes us family. Right Cousin?"

Scar Face's blood shot eyes looked like they were on fire.

Then Trevor did the talking. Trevor spoke to Scar face in the West Indian patios, and slapped him on the back. Trevor had big, heavy hands.

"Wha a gwaan, mon?" Trevor said. (What's going on man?)

"Bobby-lon, dat urt, yu nuh." (Oh officer. You make my back hurt when you slap me like that.)

＊＊＊＊＊

Drug dealers spend time and energy staying away from the police. Catching them in the act wasn't easy. Dave's team knew that they couldn't just grab their man dealing drugs. So they did the next best thing and caught him "not" in the act.

Stage two was to interrupt Scar Face's operation. Whenever Scar Face did anything that wasn't proper, the team popped up, out of the blue.

Scar Face smacked and kicked on of his workers on the corner. He moved forward to step on his underling's head, but to his surprise Ricky Radar was standing right there.

"Problem cousin?"

"Na bobby-lon, me gud."

"Sorry cousin, fighting in public is a violation of the penal code. You're going through."

Ricky quoted the statute, and arrested Scar Face and took him to the precinct. "Going through the system" entailed getting arrested, and then going downtown to see the judge. This process took about twenty-four hours.

Scar Face was lead away in cuffs; knowing he would spend the night in jail.

* * * * *

Scar Face failed to signal on a turn. Trevor asked him for a driver's license that he knew Scar Face didn't have.

Trevor spoke to Scarface in his own patois, "Yu documents nuh gud. Yu a go si di judge, mon. (You're guilty of unlicensed vehicular operation. You're going through, buddy.)"

Scar Face was lead away in cuffs; knowing he would spend the night in jail.

* * * * *

A street corner was the scene of a fiercely competitive domino game. Scar Face and his pals slammed the dominoes on their table as they laughed and cheered each other on. All of them had their money out to place bets.

Chase walked up to the table with his hat pulled down, giggling. It was his turn.

"Scar Face, are you guys waving around money while your neighbors go hungry? Public gambling for monetary profit is a misdemeanor in the penal code." He stopped for a second to let out one last chuckle. "Sorry, but you guys gotta through."

"Yu luk like yu real sorry, der, bobby-lon." (I don't believe you are as sorry as you say, officer.)

Scar Face was lead away in cuffs; knowing he would spend the night in jail.

* * * * *

The team pulled up on Scar Face one sunny afternoon. He seemed to be in the middle of something different. They were sure they had caught their man in the act of drug dealing. Money and product had been exchanged.

Scar Face was on the sidewalk at a table full of socks. He smiled broadly. "Mi jus a sell some socks, Bobby-lon."

Dave and his men looked around. Sure enough some druggies were holding up new socks. They all smiled and showed their bad teeth. A search of the area revealed nothing.

"Mi gud, Bobby-lon?"

"You got a license to sell your wares out on the streets, Scar Face?" asked Dave. "Because if you don't, you're going through."

"Weh yu seh?" (Huh?)

Scar Face was lead away in cuffs; knowing he would spend the night in jail.

* * * * *

But the last time was different.

"You got him with the goods, Trevor?" Dave asked his big officer.

"Got him, Sarge."

Dave grinned. His boys were all grown up, making collars on their own.

"Tell me about it."

"We were just going to visit him, but Ricky Radar noticed that Moshu and Dread were standing by. Then we saw Juicer," Trevor said.

Dave thought for a second. It was hard to keep up with all the nicknames. "We got Juicer last week about the same time, right?"

"Yes, with a good stash on him. We knew they were about to re-up."

Dave liked where this was going. The "stash" was the supply of drugs being sold, and "re-upping" meant a restock.

"Tell me more," said Dave.

As Trevor spoke, Dave saw it clearly. Ricky Radar sees three men step off the corner with spunk. He doesn't see Scar Face up the block, but knows the only reason these guys jump up is for their boss. A look to Johnny Mack and the police van speeds around the block. Trevor yells for them to drive faster. Chase poises himself to jump.

When they see the police van, the four men step away from the car. But the main one is a little behind—he couldn't have been near the front of the car. Ricky Radar and Chase jump out and grab him, Johnny Mack helps freeze the others, yelling to Trevor to check the back of the car....

"So how much? Don't keep me in suspense, Trevor."

"Right here. It was in the tail light." Trevor held up a big plastic bag. In it were six smaller bags. Each one had over two hundred zip-locks of crack-cocaine, packaged for sale.

Scar Face was lead away in cuffs—but this time the jail sentence he faced would be much, much more than a night in jail... he would have to exit the six-seven, stage three.

Chapter Seventeen

Donations, Donations

As the Christmas season neared, Dave was again taken by the holiday spirit. He had big plans for the first Christmas of the new millennium.

"This year's my tradition year, Vicky. Year number three."

"Why's that a tradition year, Dave?"

"Blue Christmas is way more than a re-peat. If you do something for three years in a row, then it's a tradition. Isn't it? "

"Hmm, I'm not too sure."

"Well I am. So I'm going to do things right. Everyone gives me five bucks this year."

"I thought you started getting five dollars last year."

"Yes some did, but not all. This time it's mandatory. Either that, or it's the Grinch list."

*****

Some neighborhoods are considered bad because of a high crime rate. But no matter how rough the neighborhood, most residents aren't bad at all. Cops know that it's a small percentage of the people who drive most of the crime.

The good cops go into neighborhoods and know who's who. The same old faces stand on the same old corners. Body language and facial expressions also tell stories. An experienced cop looks to see how a person reacts to the police. So if you're hanging out with someone who pays too much attention to passing police cars, get a new friend. He's up to no good.

* * * * *

Most every officer in the six-seven contributed to the Blue Christmas. But the few that didn't were the ones that caught Dave's attention. He read them just as easy as people on the streets.

He saw a certain few that dipped in another direction when he came by. He saw their facial expressions, the averting of their eyes. This attracted Dave's attention as much as a drug dealer trying to look inconspicuous. And Dave liked challenges.

* * * * *

Dave stopped by the doorway where Officer Frank Macho and Ms. Penelope Dish were about to walk out. Every precinct in the city has a couple that thinks their dating is hush-hush. They make googily eyes, or whisper to each other. But the only ones who think it's a secret are them. Every precinct? Or would that be every work place in the world?

Officer Macho wasn't the kind of person embarrassed by being called a Grinch. Dave had threatened to get a big Grinch picture and hang it from the ceiling of the muster room. Underneath it he would write a list of cops who refused to give him five dollars.

"Yeah boss, put my name on your dumb list." Macho said.

Now with Macho and his Dish together, Dave had new ammunition. Dave blocked their way and started asking questions.

"Hey Frank." Dave asked him with the most innocent look that he could muster. "How are your kids doing? Christmas coming soon?"

Family questions are nice, but not when you're standing in public with Ms. Side-Dish. Frank had to answer a question like that politely, but definitely didn't like it.

Dave leaned forward and sniffed at Frank. "Smelling good, man. What is that you're wearing?"

Dave had no intention on listening to Macho's answer. Now he caught Penelope's attention. He smiled at her.

Dave's smile has been known to be infectious. "You know, my dear, I do believe it is *you* that smells so nice, and *not* Frankie over here." Penelope Dish was all smiles.

The Macho man wasn't happy with the whole scenario Dave was painting. His personal space was being invaded.

"Hey Sarge, you know what?" Frank said. "I don't think I chipped in my five bucks for your Blue Christmas yet."

Dave ignored him and kept staring at Ms. Dish. "My, my, dear. What big eyes you have—"

Officer Macho shoved a five-dollar bill into Dave's hands. Then he took his Dish and left. He had no time for other people's sense of humor. He considered Dave a very unfunny guy.

Dave waved to the two as they left. He had already mugged several cops today. Three by intimidation, and two that had gotten pretty physical. He actually had to chase one officer the length of the precinct. But this exchange with Frankie Macho left him feeling like he had scored a knockout.

Johnny Mack had witnessed Dave's exchange.

"It's not enough to beat on them, Sarge. You've got to go hurt their feelings too," he said to Dave.

"It's for the greater good. That guy's the kind of idiot that would actually brag about not putting in five bucks."

"Yeah, he is a chump," agreed Johnny Mack.

"How about you, did you get to mug anybody today, Johnny?"

Johnny Mack's eyes glowed as he smiled. Like Dave, he also had a good day.

"Yeah," he said. "Rex and Adams helped me jump a couple of cheapos in the locker room. I ripped one of their pockets half off."

Chapter Eighteen

Operation: Blue Christmas

Neighborhoods have a way of growing on people. Especially when you work there. Drive to the same place enough times, and it starts to feel like you're coming home. Cops feel like that, too. The people in their precinct's neighborhood start to feel like family. The bad guys? That's more like distant family.

*****

Dave wasn't happy with his postal experience from a year ago. There just weren't enough letters from the six-seven. He knew his precinct, and the post office wasn't the answer. More letters could have come from their neighborhood. Any cop who patrolled there knew that. Reaching out to these kids was another matter. Dave needed to zero in on the target.

Luckily Dave knew that there were people who interacted with these kids every day. People who knew the children. People who were charged with their care five days a week.

"I've got the answer, Vicky."

"What's that Dave?"

"Teachers."

"Teachers, Dave?"

"Exactly Vicky. Teachers know what's going on."

There were a few elementary schools in the six-seven. Dave went to each of them and told them he was running a Christmas drive. Cops would deliver presents. The gifts would be inexpensive. Just the less fortunate children should go on the lists.

Dave also asked the schools to get a Santa letter from each child. He didn't want parents to think that they were being put on a "poor" list. Answering a letter gave the cops a reason to visit a house. To Dave the idea was an easy one.

Blue Christmas Lesson #6

Nothing's easy. Why would I ever think such a thing—and Vicky, why am I even thinking for myself at all?

While working with the schools, Dave soon learned that he was a fish out of water. He spoke to many school officials. He explained his plans endlessly. It was much different than dealing with cops.

Dave had no way of knowing where his message went. He didn't know these teachers personally. Was his request going to one teacher, or many? More importantly, would the right kids get picked? Dave knew that he had no control of what was sent back to him.

* * * * *

Children being children, when the letters started to come in, many asked for Play Stations and Game Boys. Some asked for bicycles, pets, computers, or other things that were impossible.

But with all the problems he had, Dave's results with the schools were better than the post office. Actually, he got more than he had ever hoped for.

Blue Christmas was going to be done right, and done right in the six-seven.

*****

Not many things intimidated Dave. A stack of letters? No problem. Volunteers needed? We've got cops. Money to buy presents? We'll get donations—and mug the Grinches. I knew Dave to be overboard, but I found it incredible that so many cops jumped right into the mix with him.

The elfin crew got the money together and bought gifts. They found a couple of wholesale toy stores to shop from, and managed to find toys that cost about five dollars or less.

There were mostly dolls for girls and toy cars for boys. There were board games for older kids. With the budget they had, it was the best they could do. They were all so proud.

The precinct elves took over a room on the second floor and started to wrap the gifts. These gifts went down to a prisoner's cell used as a giant storage closet. With all of the fuss going on, the Chief of Brooklyn South stopped by to see what was happening.

Chief Joseph Bradley was polite without trying. He always stopped and talked to officers. And chief or not, he listened to what the cops had to say. Everyone considered him to be their uncle.

"What's going on, Dave?" asked Bradley.

"Elves at work. For the Blue Christmas, Chief."

Bradley looked around the room. He saw boxes and boxes of toys, separated into piles. There was a chart on the wall matching toys to age groups. Johnny Mack and Trish supervised—they read from lists and gave out instructions. Cops took orders, wrapped and labeled gifts. Bradley nodded his head as he took it all in.

"This is quite an operation... what is it called again, Dave?"

"Blue Christmas, sir."

"Blue, blue. Blue Christmas." Bradley repeated after Dave and rubbed his chin. Dave knew the chief was bouncing the familiar phrase off of thirty somewhat years of police experience. After a moment Dave saw the slightest raise of one eyebrow, which told him the chief had made up his mind on the subject.

"Operation: Blue Christmas," Bradley said. "Very nice, sergeant. Carry on."

"Yes sir."

Chapter Nineteen

Deliveries, To The Letter

Now armed with a better set of letters, a group of elves were ready for the Blue Christmas of 2000. By getting the schoolteachers involved, the Christmas drive had evolved into a true operation.

Dave received many letters that were more humble than the ones he found at the post office.

Dear Santa Claus,
I have been good this year. I
have did my home work.
This year I wish I could have a
Barbie Doll and a winter coat.
yours truly,
Jessica

Years of anticipation could make an elf's delivery special.

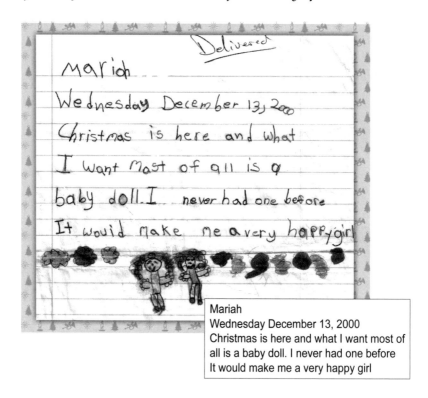

Mariah
Wednesday December 13, 2000
Christmas is here and what I want most of all is a baby doll. I never had one before
It would make me a very happy girl

Because everyone remembers their first....

On Christmas Eve of 2000 the elves turned the six-seven's muster room into a tiny North Pole. There were boxes of wrapped gifts and a hill of teddy bears. Dave sat at a table in the middle of the room with a pile of letters and addresses, readied himself to dispatch the deliveries. A group of elves got ready to help.

A loud flow of Christmas music from the rear entrance of the station house got everyone's attention. Disco Vin came in carrying a huge boom-box that looked suspiciously like it was playing an 8-track.

Vinny Vitale put the boom-box on the floor and bopped around the room. He stopped dramatically and held out his hand for a partner. All the female officers laughed and pointed. All but one.

Lisa Harbor, in full uniform like Vinny, reached out her hand. Vinny swung into action. To the other ladies' surprise, Vinny could dance! He spinned Lisa around with great skill, and showed off the footwork of a professional dancer. His big butt moved in perfect rhythm.

After this dance the other girls weren't laughing—they wanted to dance too. They lined up, each of them asking to be picked for the next dance.

Dave looked at Vinny, who was definitely out of breath. He too, wondered what the senior cop would do. Vinny pulled a comb out of his pocket, passed it through his hair, and shoved it back and threw his hand out towards another female cop. This was glory time—he would get to breathe later.

> **Delivered**
>
> Dear Santa
> For Christmas I like to have some paint to be able to paint my room cause it has not be painted for a long time even the walls are falling down. And the landlord wont do it. I would like it to be sky blue cause just waking up with my room painted skyblue I will wake up with a smile on my face, I just need the paint I could get someone to help me paint it.
> Yours truly
> Trina

Dear Santa
For Christmas I like to have some paint to be
able to paint my room cause it has not be
painted for a long time even the walls are falling
down. And the landlord wont do it. I would like
it to be sky blue cause just waking up with my
room painted skyblue I will wake up with a smile
on my face, I just need the paint I could get
someone to help me paint it.
Yours truly
Trina

Johnny Mack and Chase read the letter and wanted to help. They went to the apartment using an alleged noise complaint as an excuse to knock on the door. They took a quick look to see if any paint would help. But the walls were in such a state of disrepair that painting them would be impossible.

They asked Dave if they could do anything about it. He told them not a chance; they didn't know the family's story. Unless they had the time, money and energy to do the job themselves—they would do nothing except make the delivery.

When Johnny Mack and Chase delivered the toys, the family was grateful. The policemen put their best faces on, but each had a hollow feeling inside their stomach. They made small talk with the family. They laughed and joked with the little girl, and asked about her school grades. Because that's what real elves do.

106

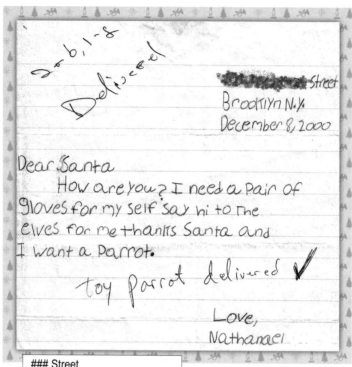

Street
Brooklyn N.Y.
December 8, 2000
Dear Santa
How are you? I need a pair of
gloves for myself say hi to the
elves for me thanks Santa and
I want a parrot.
Love,
Nathanael

You never know what kids may ask for. Trish insisted on taking this delivery herself.

"I'll deliver this one, Sarge."

"You got this one, young lady?" Dave asked.

"I insist. This one is mine."

"You want to grab some of our funds to buy the gloves?"

"No, I took this letter to one of the stores on Utica Avenue. To my Israeli friend, who has a big crush on me…" She paused for a second to smile and roll up her eyes. Then she said, "And we obviously can't blame him for that, can we?"

Dave could only smile at Trish's confidence.

Trish continued, "He loved our Blue Christmas, and was too happy to help. He gave me these."

Trish showed Dave a bag and pulled out a glove and scarf set. Then a toy parrot. Dave laughed.

"Don't worry, Sarge. I know you want to help—I'll take some of your wrapping paper."

"You go, elf-girl."

*****

"Little things…"

Dear Santa,
How are you? I am just asking you if you can please
send me a hat for my mom because she can not
afford it. I do not want my mom to get sick. I love my
mom so can you please give my mom a hat.
Love
Nayisha

Sometimes the little things aren't so little. A little thing like a hat can become so big, that it covers up the one you love.

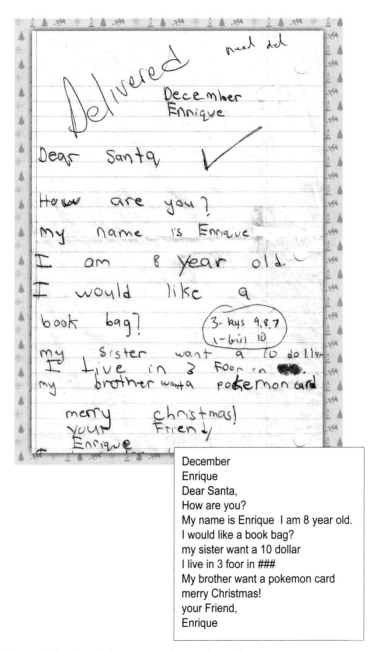

December
Enrique
Dear Santa,
How are you?
My name is Enrique I am 8 year old.
I would like a book bag?
my sister want a 10 dollar
I live in 3 foor in ###
My brother want a pokemon card
merry Christmas!
your Friend,
Enrique

Little things like book bags, cards, and pocket money aren't always taken for granted.

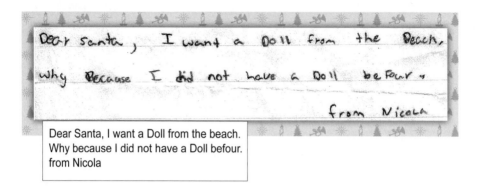

Dear Santa, I want a Doll from the beach.
Why because I did not have a Doll befour.
from Nicola

Sometimes the little things are worth writing about. Because no matter how little the wish can be, a dream is still a dream.

*****

Ricky Radar was paired with Trevor in one car; Johnny Mack and Chase were in the other. Both had big plastic garbage bags full of wrapped presents in the back seats. They met at the intersection of Church and Utica Avenues.

"Linden and East 48 Street, right?" Ricky asked Chase. "The big lady?"

"Yeah, that's the one. She's standing in the middle of the street wearing a winter coat over her pajamas." Chase said.

"She waved you guys down too? I think she's stopping every police car she sees," Johnny Mack said.

Trevor shook his head. He smiled, but he was a little upset.

"We've got to put it over the radio not to stop for her. She's too much." Trevor said. "Running after every police car out there and asking for presents. It's messing up our operation, she's too greedy— I'm telling you!"

*****

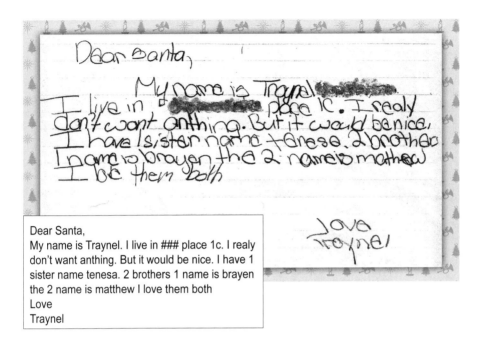

Dear Santa,
My name is Traynel. I live in ### place 1c. I realy
don't want anthing. But it would be nice. I have 1
sister name tenesa. 2 brothers 1 name is brayen
the 2 name is matthew I love them both
Love
Traynel

After going through previous disappointment, some children are careful not to get carried away. It would be wrong of them to get their hopes up. Because on an empty Christmas morning, it would be only their own feelings they'd hurt.

Traynel tries to cushion his fall by asking for a present with caution—he doesn't need anything—but, it would be nice. In case it's all right to hope, he does have a sister. And his brothers? He loves them both.

Chapter Twenty

2001... The Blue Wall

Up until the month of September, 2001 was a normal year. New York City was the Big Apple, and Brooklyn was Brooklyn.

* * * * *

In the year 2001, the world remembers New York City for what happened on September 11th. Everything else pales in comparison.

In the morning we watched the replays of a plane crashing into one of the towers on television. Information came in scattered. When the second plane hit everyone understood that we under attack.

Dave headed into the six-seven for work. He had no idea what the definition of "work" was going to be for that day. Policemen from all over the city were responding to the Trade Center. As both towers fell, "Ground Zero" took on meaning.

Dave was assigned to a stand-by post at Kings County Hospital in Brooklyn. Many emergency workers in the city who didn't go directly to ground zero went on stand-by at different locations.

Hospitals around the city set up for an overflow of patients. Thousands of people worked in the World Trade Center. Once the hospitals in Manhattan were filled, the other four boroughs would be ready to accept the wounded. Only the hospitals in Manhattan never got full.

Soon it was clear that no survivors were going to be pulled from the wreckage of the Twin Towers. The triages set up around the city sat quiet and empty.

＊＊＊＊＊

Over the next few days, weeks, and into the months, people from around the country, and even the world, became involved in the rescue and recovery effort. Like everyone else, Dave worked it while he was on-duty, and volunteered while off-duty.

The Twin Towers were made from thousands of tons of concrete, steel and glass. They stood over one hundred stories tall and had dominated the Manhattan skyline. But in the wreckage there were almost no signs of concrete or glass. "Powder" was everywhere.

Not much had survived besides the steel beams that are pictured in the wreckage of the twin towers. They say if you tried to build a frame from all of the steel recovered, you couldn't build one quarter of the original towers. The force of those buildings coming down had turned everything into dust.

＊＊＊＊＊

The inner workings of the police department went on, and Dave's hard work during the last couple of years was rewarded with a transfer up to the detective squad as a robbery sergeant in early November.

On a day in November of 2001, a mugger set his sights on a lady in an ATM bank. Like a hyena, he picked himself a small, helpless target. The petite lady, about five-foot even, was tired from a hard day's work. Her name was Anita Phillips, a cleaning lady by profession. She was someone who worked honestly for her day's pay.

Anita had just taken some cash out of the machine. The robber approached her with a knife and demanded money. Although the robber towered over her, she fought. The two struggled fiercely, bouncing off the bank's atm's and glass walls for a good five minutes.

The hyena didn't know he had picked out a lioness. She struck out, kicked, scratched, and fought back in every way she could. He was bitten four separate times. The mugger ran away without a dime. But Anita received many stitches for her efforts.

Dave and his detectives went hunting for the robber. There was a group of goons that regularly used bank fronts to solicit for one fake charity or another, or to run confidence scams. Every one of them was brought in for questioning. By night's end Dave's guys had their man.

The little lioness was asked to view a line-up. The suspect would stand along with five other persons and all six would hold up different numbers. Could she pick her assailant out?

She viewed the line-up through a two-way mirror, standing on her tiptoes to look. Both of her hands were bandaged. In a second her eyes flared and she started to scream.

"Numba four, numba four! Yu still waan mi money, numba four? Yu nuh have nuh knife now—eh! Yu likkle good-fi-nuttin tief'!"

The mugger couldn't see her through the glass. But he sure could hear her. Everyone in the building could. Not knowing what else to do, he put the number over his face. The other men laughed and pointed at him. The lioness screamed some more.

*****

Dave and his detectives spoke to Anita. They couldn't understand why she had fought. Money could be replaced. Her hands could not. Neither could her life.

She told them that she lived with her mother, who was ill. She had one child, who was nine. She had no formal education, but she made up for that by working hard. There was one person who put food on the table, and it was she.

"Offi'sas," she told them, "it was mi life mi a fight for."

A senior detective, Bobby Slayton, known to everyone as "Little Bob," asked the robbery sergeant if he could speak to her. Just short of six-foot, and well over three hundred pounds, Little Bob cut an impressive figure. Broad shoulders, big arms, and a Buddha-like belly. But a surprisingly small waist.

"Weh yu waan, deteck-tif?" She asked Little Bob, who was four times her size. The lioness had fought with a knife-wielding mugger that day, an over-sized detective didn't scare her at all.

Little Bob measured the lioness. "Fought for your life today, I understand?" His voice was deep and clear.

"Yu do understand, it was for mi chile and mi mum. I take care of 'em both."

The detective did understand, and stated exactly that. Little Bob leaned over to look at her bandaged hands. How deep were the cuts, how long it would take to heal? What had the doctors said? At first she didn't want to talk, but when she saw only concern on the detective's face, she answered him. Slowly her guard came down.

The detective asked her how her son was doing in school, and about the health of her mother. Little Bob spoke to her about his own mother, who had also raised him on her own. Like many who had grown up poor, Little Bob's memories of his father were only those at a young age.

As Little Bob spoke, Anita couldn't help but to see her reflection in his mother's life; and an image of her own child in this man's youth. She commented that his mother must be proud of him, a detective.

"Yes she was…" Little Bob said. "I miss her everyday."

Anita nodded and looked down.

Little Bob sorted through the evidence photos. They showed the cuts on Anita's hand before the doctors had worked on them. As Anita looked on, she began to realize the consequences of her actions. Slowly at first, then more noticeably, her body started to tremble.

Little Bob spoke again. How many days she would miss from work? And when she missed these days, would this time off be covered with pay? Like most people in her situation, the answer was of course, no.

The detective knew how to talk to people, and was a patient man. Over the years he had spoken to many a victim, witness, criminal. He could wait for a person to come around. He could wait for the truth. There were times when patient questioning was the only way to break a case.

Anita had been a super-woman that day. But Little Bob guided her back. He slowed her down, reminding her of the important things in her life. He helped her change back into the mother and daughter she really was. And he knew exactly when this moment had come. Then he looked her straight in her eyes, and asked one last question, gently, but firm.

"Anita, and while you were fighting with this animal, what if that knife had slipped and cut deep into your body—who then, would take care of your son and mother?"

The tears that needed to come now poured out freely.

"Oh Gawd, de-tektive, weh mi do? Yu mek it suh klear."

The lioness existed no more, there was only Anita. She folded over on her chair shaking and crying. Little Bob softly patted her back.

"Weh mi do—oh gawd, oh gawd!"

* * * * *

That night Dave told me about the robbery. For him it was the slap in the face that he needed. He realized that he had been going through the motions lately.

"I learned something today, Vicky. That lady and that perp taught me something."

"That lady—and the perp, too? What could that lesson be, Dave? One almost lost her fingers fighting over money, and the other is a robber."

"They both showed me that life goes on. No matter how bad things get. There are mothers out there that will fight to the death if their kids are threatened. And the muggers haven't missed a beat. I've got my jobs to do."

When he said "jobs" I had a good idea of where he was heading. "Does that mean you're doing Blue Christmas again this year, Dave?"

"Yes Vicky—we can't surrender."

* * * * *

Slowly but surely, over the next few months, and then over the next few years, New York City got back to normal. That most certainly happened with the police first. Cops were still needed on the streets.

Desk Officers stayed grumpy. They kept everything in order and wrote tirelessly in command logs. They took control of policemen and assignments. Just as their predecessors had always done.

* * * * *

It's been alleged that the Blue Wall is a code of loyalty among cops, a barrier put up against the outside world. But that's not the true meaning of the Blue Wall.

The real secret of the Blue Wall comes out in times of danger. Real cops back each other up, because protecting life is more important than being afraid. Those who have felt that fear, but ran in anyway, understand this. Each and every cop is a brick in the Blue Wall. Even when no one else will stand with them, police tradition calls for cops to stand together.

Whenever peril has struck the streets of the city, the Blue Wall has stood in tact. Sometimes even at the cost of policemen's lives. This will always be the case, today, tomorrow—for all the September 10[th's], 11[th's], and 12[th's] ever to come.

Chapter Twenty-One

Delivering Strong

While the police department continued with its recovery effort at Ground Zero, many kids in the city lived their day-to-day lives without change. The elves of the six-seven knew this. They too, refused to change their yearly habits because of 9/11. They delivered strong.

Do you really know what everyone in your family wants for Christmas? This little girl has a clear handle on her family's wants and needs.

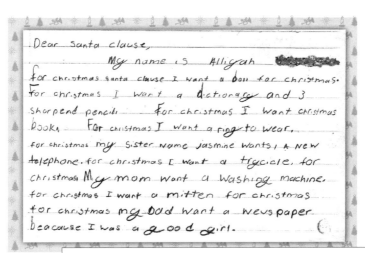

Dear Santa clause,
My name is Alliyah. For Christmas santa clause I want a doll for Christmas. For Christmas I want a dictionary and 3 sharpend pencils. For Christmas I want Christmas book. For Christmas I want a ring to wear. For Christmas my sister name jasmine wants a new telephone. for Christmas I want a trycicle. for Christmas My mom want a washing machine. for Christmas I want a mitten for Christmas for Christmas my Dad want a newspaper. because I was a good girl.

When in doubt…

I wa cat
Dea Santa,
Jennifer

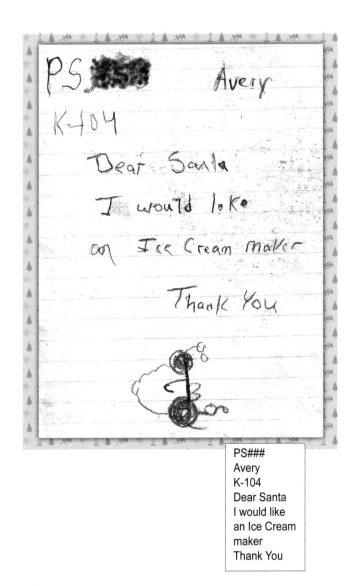

PS###
Avery
K-104
Dear Santa
I would like
an Ice Cream
maker
Thank You

…draw it out.

Brooklyn N.Y. 11208
December 8

Dear Santa,

I want to tell you that this Christmas my Parents do not have any money. I am writing you this letter because I want to get a pairs of new bedroom Slippers for my mother, My Aunt and my Grandma. I would like some socks for my Uncle and my baby brother Tariq.

Love,
Keeosha

Dear Santa,
I want to tell you that this Christmas my parents do not have any money. I am writing you this letter because I want to get a pairs of new bedroom slippers for my mother, My Aunt and my Grandma. I would like some socks for my Uncle and my baby brother Tariq.
Love,
Keesha

Sometimes the kids wished with special letters. What made a letter so special? When kids ask not for themselves, but for others.

Dave and his elves went to the stores and shopped for these 'special' wishes.

Chase looked at the letter and said to Dave, "C'mon Sarge, this kid's asking for slippers and socks—we've gotta come through for her!"

Dave nodded his head and showed the letter to Trish, "Is that store owner from Utica Avenue still in love with you?"

Trish struck a pose putting one leg in front of another and placing both of her hands on her hips. "And how could he not?"

"Of course. Thank goodness for pride and vanity. Can you take this letter over there, please?"

* * * * *

As in the previous years, some of the kids' requests were just way over the cops' heads.

Dear Santa,
Santa all I want for Christmas is my Daddy. I want to see my daddy. I want my daddy to come home with me, my family, and my mommy too.
I want my daddy to be with my mom. If we are sick Santa my will be there. I want momy and my brother and Father to be with me forever.
From Shaniya

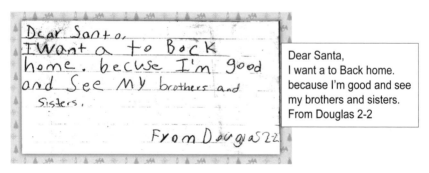

Dear Santa,
I want a to Back home. because I'm good and see my brothers and sisters.
From Douglas 2-2

When the elves saw letters like this, they wished the kids would go back to asking for play-stations and computers. So it would feel better when they couldn't deliver.

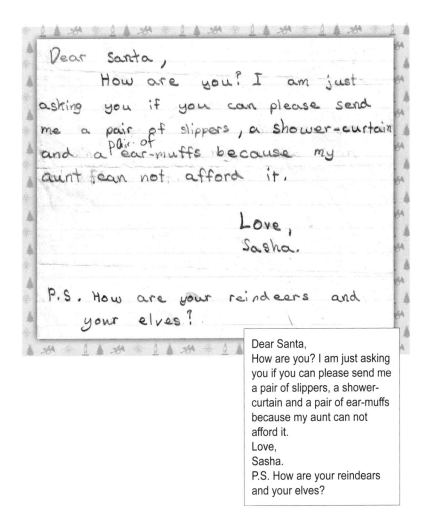

Dear Santa,
How are you? I am just asking you if you can please send me a pair of slippers, a shower-curtain and a pair of ear-muffs because my aunt can not afford it.
Love,
Sasha.
P.S. How are your reindears and your elves?

Have you ever dealt with kids who feel that you owe them presents? You know the kind. But they're really not ungrateful, they're just kids. But there are some kids know that asking for something might seem impolite. That's why kids with good manners first ask how Santa is doing. And when they do ask for presents, it is also polite to give the reasons of why they are asking in the first place. Lastly, they ask about the things that are important to you... so they don't sound ungrateful.

Dave left the squad's office for a while to cruise around with Trevor and Ricky Radar. They stopped at a house by East 32 Street.

A man answered the door. His face was red from years of alcohol abuse. The odor didn't just come from his mouth, but from his whole body.

Ricky looked at Dave and asked why they were stopping here. He and Trevor had given presents to this house already. Dave told him that there had been a homicide on this street last summer. There were rumors that the murderer was seen recently.

"Yes, officers, you have my presents?" The drunken man addressed the three policemen.

"We're just checking up that you got them, sir." Dave pulled out a wanted photo from his pocket and showed it to the man. "Have you seen this guy around here? There's a reward for him."

The man didn't look at the picture. "My kids," he said. "My kids, what about my kids?"

He pointed at four children inside the doorway. The youngest must have been two years old. The oldest looked to be about eight. Old enough to feel embarrassed. Behind the kids was a big Christmas tree, in a well-furnished apartment.

Ricky told the man, "All of your kids got presents from us. Not that you needed them. Did you call the precinct or did your wife?"

"My wife is working, I called. Because the baby didn't get a toy."

"The baby got a bear. That's what we give babies." Ricky said. "So, you work nights, and your wife works days, man?"

"I can't work, I got disabilities."

Trevor was about to reply, but Dave cut him off. The three left.

"That was my fault," Dave said to them. "I looked for something back, I was wrong."

"You were trying to do the right thing, Sarge," Ricky cut in.

"No, wrong is never right," answered Dave.

Blue Christmas Lesson #7

Real gift-givers never
ask for anything back.

The three cops didn't bring up the drunken man anymore. They knew his story. Troublesome husbands, uncles, cousins were used by families for the little bit of help they could provide. In this case the man was used to take care of the kids. Eventually they all messed up. The trouble they cause would soon outweigh their usefulness. And out they went.

*****

Dear Santa,

On Christmas, may I have a full size, green comforter set for my mom please! I feel sorry that she buys me beautiful things for my bed but not for herself. Please Santa, beg you to get this gift for her this Christmas. I am doing good in school but I am trying to do better. I would do anything to get this gift. I think she deserves it because she is always making sure my brother and I get what we need.

*Brian

Love from,
Street Bryan
Brooklyn, NY 11203

Dear Santa,
On Christmas, may I have a full size, green comforter set for my mom please! I feel sorry that she buys me beautiful things for my bed but not for herself. Please Santa, beg you to get this gift for her this Christmas. I am doing good in school but I am trying to do better. I would do anything to get this gift. I think she deserves it because she is always making sure my brother and I get what we need.
Love from,
Bryan

Chase looked at the letter and fell in love with another kid he never met. "Man this is a nice kid—where'd that Trish go? Trish— Trish! One more letter, sweetie—c'mon, take me to the store so we can get this comforter!"

* * * * *

The winter of 2001 was the mildest winter NYC had seen in a long while. It was as if the weather decided to take it easy on the people working in the wreckage looking for their friends.

All around the city, scarcely unaffected by what had happened only a few miles away, kids still dared to hope. In a precinct in Brooklyn a few elves made their stand by doing their yearly chores.

New York City's status as the Big Apple was on a time-out. But Brooklyn, was still Brooklyn.

Chapter Twenty-Two

Promise to Chase

On a cold, clear night in Brooklyn, a lone figure ran down the street, darting from side to side. In addition to exercise, he picked up a dime here, a penny there. But it was nothing like the three quarters from the night before—a real score.

Chase looked around as he jogged, but it seemed that small bits of glass were the only things shiny. I've got to get a job, he told himself. The hunger pains kicked in, but he'd be all right. He had fifty-eight cents, enough to get his little sister a pair of cupcakes. For himself, water would have to do.

The thought of his sister asking their cousins for food bothered Chase. So did his father remarrying and leaving them. His mom leaving years before was okay—she never was the motherly type. But Chase knew thinking about things he couldn't change wasn't any help. He had to get himself a job. If he had a bike he could do a paper route. He told the man that he could run it, but the man had said, "No bike, no route."

*****

A rookie cop got into formation right before roll call and smiled to himself. Chase had six bucks in hand. Christmas had put a hurt on his credit card, but he was on time with the rest of his bills, and tomorrow was payday. He'd have the five-dollar sandwich special at the deli, *and* a cup of coffee tonight. Sometimes a man couldn't help but to be proud.

A shot in the arm brought the rookie out of his spell. He thought he got hit by a truck. He looked up to see it was a heavy-handed sergeant going down the lines in two-fisted fashion. He grabbed the five-dollar bill right out of the rookie's hand.

"Thank-you, and welcome to Blue Christmas, kid," Dave told him. It was the first time the two had met.

Two other cops managed to give in five-dollar bills before getting punched. The sergeant was rough, but no one complained. At least not out loud. The rook knew he shouldn't question a boss, but that sandwich was on his mind.

"Hey Sarge," that's all I got till payday, mind if I give you five tomorrow?" the rookie asked.

"Of course I mind—I'll have to catch you again," Dave answered. "Do I look like I have time to waste? Christmas is around the corner."

Chase nodded as Dave waved over two other cops. He could see that Dave wasn't a patient man, especially when it came to other people's money. While the cops walked over, Dave gave the rookie another tidbit.

"It means more to give when you don't have." Dave looked the new cop in the eyes, "Don't you know that, rookie?"

Now with the other two cops in front of him, Dave held Rex's ten-dollar bill in his hand. The tall officer was looking for change. Nick Adams didn't have the five dollars on him. Instead he was giving a story that Dave had no interest in hearing.

"So Nicky, you're telling me that you're good for five dollars tomorrow?"

"Hmmm." Dave now looked at the Rex. "You think he's good for the money tomorrow?"

"Sure Sarge, he's *my partner*—he's good for it."

"Good, you just put in his money. *You* get five dollars from him tomorrow." Dave gave Rex a wink. "Don't worry big guy, he's good for it."

The three officers stood with their mouths open as Dave walked away with their money. But Dave was a mugger who cared. He turned back to ask a question.

"Blue Christmas, fellas?"

The three cops looked at each other. Conflict with this sergeant wasn't a good thing. They all nodded back and gave Dave back the answer he was looking for, "Sure Sarge, Blue Christmas."

Chase had no idea what a Blue Christmas was, but he'd always look back on that day as the first time he got "elf'd."

*****

A fourteen-year old ran out of his uncle's house, hungry and upset. He wasn't the kind to complain, and he never cried. But when his little sister had called Chase her "hero" over a pair of cupcakes, he had to run outside.

Chase looked up and swore that if he ever had kids he'd starve himself before they'd ever know hunger. And that he'd never cry again, because his sister shouldn't see that. And by next week, he would have himself a job. As if on cue, a blurry group of stars blinked for him. Something inside him felt acknowledged.

His tears and hunger stopped, as if his promise had sealed them up. Chase never saw those blurry group of stars again.

* * * * *

In the muster room of the six-seven, Trish handed two little boys a list. They laughed as they raced to get it filled.

Dave looked at Chase's boys and smiled. "Brought your kids again this year, Chase? You guys really get into the Blue Christmas."

"Wouldn't have it any other way Sarge," Chase replied, "even though you left us."

"I'm still here, buddy. Upstairs with the detectives, yes—but it is the same building."

Chase, on the conditions team, missed Dave the most. Chase considered Dave a cross between a big brother and a father. They left the kids with Trish to get a cup of coffee at the diner.

* * * * *

"What's wrong Chase, you look a little down."

"Nah, just thinking about my boys, I think they're spoiled. Getting fat, even."

"Good. They're only young once," Dave said.

"Yeah, but young and chunky isn't good."

"They're not that bad, Chase. Why don't you take them running with you?"

"Yeah I'd like—but they never want to." Chase smiled, but he looked sad.

"Really? You'd think it'd be in their blood. When did you start?"

"When I was fourteen."

"Good age, any special reason, like to join a sports team?"

"Just to cover more ground, really."

"More ground? What's that mean?"

"Ah nothing." Something in Chase's head clicked, and he smiled for real now. "Did I ever tell you about the time I only had six bucks on me, and got mugged for five?"

* * * * *

At night, in his home, the rookie wondered about becoming a cop, only to get mugged. Chase checked on his boys as they slept comfortably in their room. He wanted to sleep too, but he was so hungry his stomach was making noises. He thought to himself he couldn't remember when last he had been this hungry. His stomach kicked in protest, and somehow it sounded like a bell in his head.

Chase ran to the window to look outside. The night was clear, cold, and he knew what he would see. As he looked out the window he repeated to himself what the Sarge had told him earlier that day, how it means more to give when you don't have it.

He knew exactly the last time he felt so hungry—he was fourteen years old, right before he got his first job. Outside the window a familiar group of blurry stars blinked for Chase. They had been there all along. As he stared, his stomach made a noise so loud that he couldn't help but to laugh. Because he was hungry, but his kids weren't. And then, for no particular reason, Chase felt a slight tickle on his cheek, and the taste of salt on his lips.

Chapter Twenty-Three

Teefin and Robbin'

Dave continued his career as a robbery sergeant in the year of 2002. He still worked in the six-seven, but now he was "upstairs" with the detectives. It was a big move in the direction of eventually becoming a detective lieutenant, like Columbo.

"Offisah, de teefin me ere."

"Excuse me, sir?"

"I say de robbin' me, dam-mit."

* * * * *

Detectives have their own pecking order. In the six-seven, junior detectives worked robberies, and then moved in with the regular squad after they got some experience.

The detective squad of the six-seven had its share of notable "Bobs." The massive "Little Bob" Slayton was a squad fixture. Little Bob's old partner was "Bobcat" DeWitt. Bobcat had since retired, but his legend remained. "Big Bob" was the newest Bob to make the squad, but he was very quickly becoming a Bob of noteworthiness.

* * * * *

Detective Bob Guthrie was the most senior of the junior detectives. He first started as "Angry Bob." But the detectives of the squad only recognized him as "Big Bob."

Big Bob was about five foot ten, two hundred and forty pounds. He looked like a barrel. His massive chest and shoulders had dwarfed his waist as a teenager, cutting an impressive figure. Now in his late twenties, his waistline had caught up to his upper girth.

Every few weeks Big Bob would make a pledge to himself and hit the gym like a madman. He'd walk around posing with his big arms and made fun of anyone who didn't exercise. But then he would hurt his shoulder, or quit for another reason. During the times of his non-work out phases, Big Bob made fun of everyone who exercised. He pointed out that working out could do nothing for their faces.

*****

Lieutenant Antonio Russo was every bit of an Italian who grew up in Bay Ridge, Brooklyn. He was six-foot one and wore his hair combed back, slicked with gel. He spoke fast and furious; and whenever he made a point worth noting, he finished his sentence with "ba-da-bing."

Junior detective Albert Castillo, "AC," walked into the boss's office, where Lieutenant Russo was writing on a folder. He looked up for a second and gave AC a file.

"Hey AC, give this to Bob."

"Big Bob or Little Bob?"

"Big Bob."

"Hey Lieu, isn't it strange that Little Bob is bigger than Big Bob?"

"So?"

"So then why is he *Little* Bob?"

"Seniority. Little Bob had a partner named Bob—Old Bob." Russo thought for a second as his fingers drummed away on the desk, "Bobcat!" he said, "Bobcat Dewitt."

"So Little Bob and Old Big Bob were partners?"

"No Little Bob and Old Bobcat were partners. Old Bobcat Dewitt retired."

"Old Bob was bigger than Little Bob?"

"No. But he was *senior* to Little Bob." Russo pointed at the junior detective to emphasize his point. "Little Bob got named 'Little' because Old Bob was *senior* to him—ba-da-bing."

"But Little Bob is *senior* to Big Bob, *and* he's *bigger* than Big Bob."

Now Russo stopped writing and looked up at the impertinent junior detective. He couldn't believe the conversation was still going after he ba-da-bing'd him.

"So what's your point, AC?" he asked.

"So why isn't 'Big' Bob named 'Little' Bob?"

Russo leaned forward and spoke deliberately. "Because *that* name is already taken."

This time he pointed to the door, giving AC his cue to leave. As the young detective walked out, Russo looked back down at his paperwork. "Ba-da-bing," he muttered under his breath.

*****

"Call them back, call them back!" Big Bob Guthrie was screaming on the phone to an employee in a Chinese restaurant.

Dave listened over his shoulder. Big Bob yelled into the phone again, "tell them you'll deliver!"

Dave grabbed the keys and headed down to the car. Big Bob got his junior partner, AC, out of the bathroom.

"Stop with the mess, we've got to go!" Big Bob yelled. "The Chinese guy says he got a call from those punks who robbed him before—it's the same phone number. Let's go already!"

"Okay, I'm coming."

"Would you stop fiddling and c'mon!"

"Jeeze."

In the squad car Big Bob was angry.

"Did you see that Sarge? None of those old geezers got up to help." Big Bob was referring to the senior detectives. "It's a live robbery."

"We didn't ask them for help, Big Bob." AC said. "We just ran out."

"Whose side are you on, rookie?" Big Bob scowled.

Big Bob was always angry at something. But for this particular job, Dave knew he had more than enough manpower.

＊＊＊＊＊

The deliveryman stood in front of the address and rang the bell. No one answered the door. AC stood down the block pretending to tie his shoe. Dave sat on a stoop about ten houses the other way.

Two young men came running up the block with their sights set on the deliveryman. They had come for easy prey.

As Dave and AC got ready to move, they heard the screeching of tires, the sound of a car door opening, angry cursing. There was a short scuffle, and then more cursing. They ran to the car from different sides.

The skid marks could be traced from the middle of the street, onto the sidewalk, and through the grass of a front lawn. A bush was caught under the unmarked police car.

Dave and AC came up to help, but Big Bob had the two muggers on the ground already handcuffed. The robbers looked up in terror. Big Bob flexed his biceps and yelled out the merits of exercise and good behavior.

*****

It wasn't everyday that robbers got caught in the act. A couple of the older detectives from the regular squad congratulated AC. They were impressed with the catch of a live robbery. Things like that usually took time to set up.

"Would you look at that, Sarge?" Big Bob said to Dave. "You and I do all the work, and that neophyte gets all the credit."

"He did fine, Big Bob. He followed your lead," Dave was proud that the senior detectives acknowledged the good arrest.

Big Bob made a face like he just thought of something smart. He joined in on the conversation.

"Don't be modest AC, tell them how you got in the white clothes and did the delivery."

"Oh really?" asked Little Bob Slayton. "You didn't tell us about that. So you did the delivery, AC?"

"Yes he did," said Big Bob. "And kept the food. The wings were a little spicy, but the rest was delicious."

"Oh you got some food?" Now another senior detective, Mark Redding, or "Red," was interested.

AC knew he was being set up. But there was nothing he could do.

"Yeah, the store is giving us a whole big bag," continued Big Bob. "They were so thankful. I'll start the paperwork for you, AC. You go get the food. Let's share it with the men."

"Thanks AC, that's all right," said Little Bob.

The senior detectives were now open to conversation. The young boys had made a good arrest and were bringing in food. Little Bob and Red remembered when Detective Carlo Viola had delivered pizza to catch some robbers. And when Red was the local cab driver for three months, working as a decoy to catch another robbery crew. The senior detectives were a wealth of stories and information—when they actually spoke to the junior detectives.

"How did you pull off being Chinese, AC?" Red asked. "You're pretty tall. And you're tan-skinned."

"He wore a hat and bent over," Big Bob jumped in again. "Why don't you show them your delivery walk, AC? Little, little steps." Big Bob bent over with his hands out, and pretended he was pulling a rickshaw, taking tiny steps.

AC looked around. But there he was no help. The senior detectives were comparing this arrest to legendary stories. They were talking freely, about food and police work. He was stuck buying Chinese food for the office, and he had better not be stingy.

Chapter Twenty Four

Double Blue

Dave, the rookie transit cop, stood in front of his Desk Officer, Sergeant Taylor. He had gone around the clock on a stolen property arrest from the night before. Instead of taking it easy on his next tour, Dave was at the desk with another arrest.

Sergeant Taylor had been waiting all day to see the young officer.

"I looked up that oscilloscope in an electronics catalogue today, Dave. It cost three hundred dollars, not a thousand."

"Really, Sarge? I thought they were a lot more expensive than that."

"You went and got sixteen hours of overtime, on three hundred dollar's worth of equipment. It would have been cheaper for the city just to pay for it. You're a transit cop, anyway. What do you even *care* about oscilloscopes?"

Dave didn't blink. "Guess you're right there, Sarge," he said, "Good thing I got a complainant."

Dave grabbed a prisoner's pedigree form and started filling it out.

"You got a *complainant?*"

Finding the owner of the oscilloscope would have been nearly impossible. But this officer had found the complainant. The sergeant wanted to hear how Dave tracked him down.

"You actually *found* the owner?"

"Nah, Sarge, couldn't find him. I got Pathmark to press charges." Dave smiled with pride.

The sergeant was confused. "Pathmark makes oscilloscopes?"

"No Sarge, but they owned that shopping cart the guy was pushing. Clearly a case of stolen property."

The Desk Officer's jaw dropped. He couldn't believe he was having this conversation. He told his assistant that his wife had a hand in this. She had sent this rookie here to drive him crazy. He stared at Dave with measured anger and grabbed his cigar.

After a few puffs, Taylor asked Dave, "So what do you have now?"

"A turnstile jumper. Theft of service, non-payment of fare."

Dave finished the prisoner's pedigree form and handed it to Taylor with a big smile. Anyone watching would think Dave was giving him a check.

The sergeant wasn't amused.

"Write him a summons and get him out of here," he said.

"Can't Sarge, he's got warrants."

"Warrants, huh? How many?"

"One hundred and fifty-two."

* * * * *

In late October of 2002 Dave was promoted to lieutenant. It meant that he would have to leave his beloved six-seven.

The neighborhood of Crown Heights was just a couple of miles north of the six-seven. Not much more than a square mile, the 77th precinct had a legacy of its own. Dave was back in Brooklyn North, and in another heavy house.

The six-seven is a residential neighborhood full of unattached and semi-attached houses, but the seven-seven is more urban. Its blocks are lined with three and four story brownstones. The seven-seven has more apartment buildings within its boundaries, and more densely populated.

The question on Dave's mind was whether or not to introduce the seven-seven to the Blue Christmas concept. By coming to the seven-seven in November, Dave didn't have time to get to know the cops before Christmas. Getting money from strangers wouldn't be an easy task. He knew he could keep it going in the six-seven being only a couple miles away. But the seven-seven, what to do?

"I don't know, Vicky, there are a couple of different ways this thing could go. What do you think I should do?"

"Isn't that the question, Dave? What *should* you do?"

✳ ✳ ✳ ✳ ✳

Dave stepped into a supervisor's meeting a week into November. He and two new sergeants were introduced to their fellow bosses in the seven-seven. The commanding officer, Russell O'Keefe, knew Dave from the six-seven. He had done a short stint there as an executive officer.

Dave was formally introduced to his colleagues. He knew supervisor's meetings came around only once a month or two. It was now or never.

"Inspector O'Keefe, I want to announce to my fellow supervisors that I'll run the Blue Christmas at the seven-seven this year. As you know, I've been running it in the six-seven for years."

"Eh, okay Dave."

O'Keefe had not worked in the six-seven during Christmas time, and had no idea what Dave was talking about. He knew Dave as a no-nonsense sergeant. "Blue Christmas" sounded official enough.

That "okay" was all Dave needed. "Thanks for the support, inspector." Dave got up and went to each supervisor in the room. "Five dollars, please."

The inspector and his staff watched in amazement as Dave took money from everyone in the room. The Inspector started to get his wallet out but Dave waved him off. He wondered about that for a moment, and then got back to his meeting.

Two new sergeants walked out of the meeting at a loss. One asked a veteran sergeant of the seven-seven, "Hey does that happen at every CO's meeting? I just got mugged."

The veteran sergeant, Jamal Spence, shook his head. "That guy really did work the room." Spence rubbed his chin as he reviewed the matter in his mind. "Yeah, I heard he used to be a robbery sergeant. It makes sense."

*****

Inspector O'Keefe was a man trying to make changes. He had been the commanding officer of the seven-seven for about six months. He wasn't from Brooklyn North's "old school." A new lieutenant like Dave, who had Brooklyn North experience, could help him out. Especially with his background. He was happy to have Dave on his staff, even though he wasn't too sure about what just happened in his meeting.

The third platoon mustered up for roll call. O'Keefe addressed them. He had a lot of issues to deal with. There were burglaries in the east end of the precinct. Illegal social clubs had popped up on Nostrand Avenue. Kids were getting mugged outside the local high school. A rookie cop had lost his radio and whoever found it was yelling obscenities over the air. If any cop could catch that maniac, the C.O. promised them an extra day off.

The Brooklyn North cops stood stone-faced as the inspector spoke. It was all old news, and they couldn't care less. Then he introduced the two new sergeants and lieutenant.

Dave stepped forward with a big smile and hello. Then he introduced Blue Christmas. The inspector watched as Dave made the announcement. Dave told them that he expected five dollars from everyone. Whoever worked Christmas Day and Eve would be expected to pitch in.

The faces of the cops didn't have the same look as when the inspector spoke. Now some looked confused. Their personal space had been invaded. They whispered questions to each other while Dave stood at the podium.

Who was this lieutenant? What was this Blue Christmas he was talking about? Was this a part of the NYPD that they hadn't heard about? Did he really think he was going to take *their* money?

The inspector smiled. If nothing else, his new lieutenant was going to break the status quo. He started to walk out of the muster room. Dave stopped him.

"Just a minute, inspector."

"Yes, Dave?"

"Five dollars, Sir."

The inspector saw why Dave had waved him off earlier. "Okay Dave, here you go. For the Blue Christmas."

Officer AJ Mooney was a union delegate standing roll call. A lot of his cops were going to complain. He knew it, and he knew the lieutenant knew it. Shaking down the inspector right in front of the troops was a clear message that no one was off-limits. AJ had already heard about the bosses getting mugged in their meeting.

AJ watched the new lieutenant stand roll call with a broad smile. He also saw how the man's eyes didn't quite match the grin. His fellow cops didn't understand what was happening. The veteran officer had picked up on what the younger cops hadn't. AJ winced. A wolf was sizing up the sheep.

* * * * *

Officer Donny Lawson stared at his new lieutenant with annoyance. He was a fifteen-year veteran of Brooklyn North's seven-seven. He was the first to tell anyone that he worked in the toughest precinct. But he was the last person to make an arrest. Donny always looked tired.

Over the years Donny's bosses had told him things like, "It's more work trying to avoid work, Donny." Or, "it could be worse, Donny, you could have a shovel in your hands, and *really* have to work for a living."

Donny stood in front of his new lieutenant. He had work to do.

"You can't do this, Lieu. You've got a list of everyone's names and you're crossing them off? That's not right, people give when they're asked over here."

"Not according to my list. And I believe that you're one of the Grinches," Dave said.

"Grinch? I gotta stand on principle here. I'm not going to be bullied into a donation. Are you *ordering* me to put in five dollars, lieutenant?"

"You know I can't do such a thing. But if *you* don't want to put in any money, then *you* can't deliver any gifts."

Donny looked at Dave. He scraped his fingernails over his unshaven face. He knew the lieutenant's reputation for toughness. But the warning of not delivering presents made him wonder—what kind of threat was that?

AJ Mooney brought a few coffees into the precinct for the guys at the desk. He did this every day after roll call like clockwork. Donny knew this and had planned his conversation with Dave accordingly.

"Hey Mooney," Donny said, "I think we have a union issue here."

"A *union* issue?" AJ stepped cautiously into the conversation.

Donny's voice got louder. "Yes, my delegate. What do you think of a lieutenant shaking down police officers for five dollars?"

"Well I don't know if we'd call that a shake-down, would we Lieu?" AJ said.

"Call it what you want, AJ," Dave replied. "Call your union bosses, call the press. I'm sure everyone would want to know that the cops in the seven-seven don't want to give up five dollars for kids in the neighborhood."

"Yeah, let's call the union brass," said Donny, now grinning with a cup of coffee in his hand.

"Take it easy, Donny," AJ said. "I don't really think it's a *union issue*." He grabbed the officer to the side and angrily whispered, "If word got out that we're this cheap, we're going to look like idiots. You've got to pick your fights, Donny!"

"But AJ, this guy is mugging us. You're going to let a *boss* do this?"

"Most of the cops gave in the money already. They don't have a problem with this." Donny gave a stupid look. AJ continued, "I've got plenty of cops saying they're going to be elves this Christmas."

Lawson couldn't believe it. "Brooklyn North cops? *Elves?*"

AJ told Lawson to take a walk. He'd speak to him later. He looked back at Dave.

"It's not a union issue boss, so we'll talk later?"

"Well, since we're talking union, let's talk about this other list I've got."

Dave had some paperwork in his hand. He and AJ looked over the list together.

"You see, AJ," Dave continued, "Some of our officers are low on arrest activity."

"Hard to believe, Lieu."

"Yes it is. This being an A-House and all. Then, we also have a burglary problem in these three sectors."

The delegate nodded his head, but didn't like where it was going.

"Do you see all the shopping carts around this neighborhood?" Dave asked.

"Shopping carts? Like the can collectors? I don't get what you're talking about, Lieu."

Dave explained to the delegate that all of those shopping carts were stolen. And the loot from the local burglaries was most likely being carried off in these carts. Dave would start an initiative. They would fight the burglary condition by taking care of the little things. Like shopping carts. And who better to help, than the people with low arrest activity. That would be killing two birds with one stone.

"Boss eh, good plan there. I think. But we don't need to talk about this, because it really ain't a union issue. You know?"

"AJ, I expect you to help me out here, with the Blue Christmas. You'll be a good elf."

"Sure thing boss. I'll be whatever you want. Just keep me away from the shopping carts. *Please.*"

Chapter Twenty-Five

Blue, Times Two

Christmas Eve and Day of 2002 saw two precincts working hard on their Blue Christmas Operations. The six-seven was up and running as per usual. The seven-seven cops were enjoying their first Blue Christmas.

* * * * *

Tell me all about yourself in a hundred words or less…

Dear Santa,
My name is Felicia. I am 9 years old. I live at 319 ###. I would like to have a doll with long braiding hair because I would like to braid hair. When I grow up. I have 1 brother 1 sister My brother is 7 My sister is 12 years old. I like to do work. My favorite subject is English. I am neat. I also like to braid hair. My favorite food is chicken I like to sing Christmas carols and videos. I also like to dance and play double dutch. I am smart and I had a good report card.
Love, Felicia

Dave checked in on Big Bob and AC, while they delivered presents to an apartment. Bib Bob was doing push-ups with two giggling kids on his back. They looked to be about five and three years old.

"How's it going?" asked Dave.

"First time I've seen Grumpy smile so much," AC answered.

Dave looked and nodded at the two small children. Their older brother was twelve-years old, and impressed with the show, and mom was laughing.

Big Bob told the twelve-year old to get on too. After a little coaxing, the bigger kid stepped onto Big Bob's back. The detective knocked of twenty push-ups with all three kids on his back. Everyone clapped together each time he came up.

Big Bob got up to go, red in his face from pushing it a little too much. The kids wanted him to stay, but he needed to get some air.

"Okay kids, behave this year. Listen to your mom, and be good in school."

The three policemen got up to go but the five-year old stopped Big Bob with a tug on his pant leg.

"Big Bob, will you come see us next year, too? We didn't see you last year."

Big Bob couldn't speak for a second. He pictured what it must have been like a year before. Promises were easy to make, but much easier to break. There was no way of knowing where any of them would be a year from now. He knew he could make that promise, but wasn't sure if he could deliver. In his mind Big Bob pictured a kid waiting by the door for him, for a visit that might or might not come.

"I'll try to," said Big Bob. Real elves had to strong enough to lie to little children, but even with his big arms, Big Bob wasn't strong enough to be a good elf.

"Hey man," the twelve year old grabbed his brother, "let's not talk about last year and next year when we've got this year right here. Don't stress the Dee-Tee's (detectives), little brother."

Big Bob mouthed the words "thank you" to the little man, and then walked out. He got into the car with his head looking down. AC shrugged. He knew his partner would be grumpy again.

A book-bag, $7.99, a hat, $5.99, a new doll, $6.99. …Second-graders learning the value of a budget, and how to stretch a dollar: priceless.

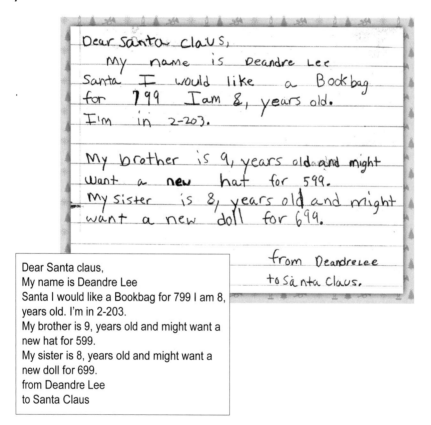

Dear Santa claus,
My name is Deandre Lee
Santa I would like a Bookbag for 799 I am 8, years old. I'm in 2-203.
My brother is 9, years old and might want a new hat for 599.
My sister is 8, years old and might want a new doll for 699.
from Deandre Lee
to Santa Claus

Another writer with a flair for math. If you look closely you'll see a boy who dares to dream with large numbers, and who doesn't neglect his reading, either.

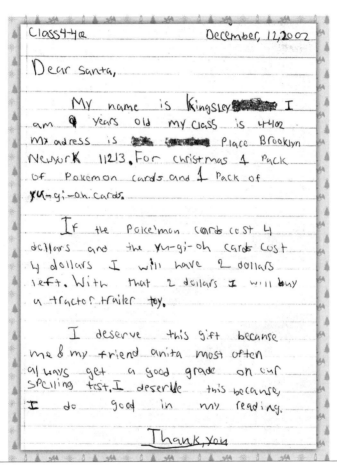

Class 4-402   December, 12, 2002
Dear Santa,
My name is Kingsley. I am 9 years old my class is 4-402 My address is #### Place Brooklyn NewYork 11213. For Christmas 1 pack of Pokemon cards and 1 pack of yu-gi-oh cards.
If the pokemon cards cost 4 dollars and the yu-gi-oh cards cost 4 dollars I will have 2 dollars left. With that 2 dollars I will buy a tractor trailer toy.
I deserve this gift because me & my friend anita most often get a good grade on our spelling test, I deserve this because, I do good in my reading.
Thank you

This letter was forwarded to the child's mother. Yet another burden placed on a single working mother's back.

[forward to mother]
P.S.   David   Class 30 Dec.17, 2002   Christmas letter   ### st   Brooklyn NY
Dear Saint Nick,
This Christmas I would like to have a little time to spend with my mother. You see my mother is always working during the week. Her only day off is on Monday. On that day all she wants to do is rest and sleep. My mother is very tired when she comes home. All I want to do have a little fun with my mother. We can go to places like the theater or to a buffet where we can eat till we drop. However I can understand if you cannot do this for me. I'm just asking because I love my mother.
Sincerally David

* * * * *

On Christmas Day Dave scooted over to the six-seven to meet up with his regular elves. Trevor, Ricky Radar, and Chase were all in a doughnut shop. Cops like doughnut shops for their good coffee. Dave sat down with the boys.

"How's the lieutenant business?" asked Trevor, chewing on a jelly doughnut.

"Usual stuff." Dave looked at the door, and saw a man and a woman standing outside the doughnut shop. They were panhandling, and looked familiar.

"You recognize them, Lieu?" Chase asked, as he chomped down a glazed doughnut.

Of course Dave did. In a way, they had helped introduce him to the six-seven. The two were residents of the Veer. Somewhat. They had moved in years ago, got evicted, but never moved out. Just around. They managed to find vacated apartments within the complex and moved into them until they got kicked out of those. They were friendly people, who happened to have a few problems.

"Bring them in here, Trevor." Dave said.

Trevor walked up to Cindy and Mo. "Why are you two panhandling here on Christmas?"

"Merry Christmas, Trevor," Cindy said. "Mo and I have a couple of nieces in the Vandeveer, you know. We're saving up to get them something for Christmas." Mo grunted in agreement.

Trevor's eyes went wide as he looked back to his partners. "You hear these two? They're saving up for Christmas—*on Christmas!*"

"Now Trevor, you don't have to try and embarrass us in front of Lieutenant Dave like that. Isn't that right, Ricky?" Again Mo grunted in agreement.

All the cops were amazed how Cindy and Mo could always keep track of all their names and ranks. The group put their heads together to discuss what to do.

Trevor brought doughnuts and hot chocolate over to the couple. Then he gave them gifts for their little nieces.

"Now listen to me," he said, "take these presents straight to your nieces. We will come check on you later, I promise."

"You're so sweet, boys," Cindy said. Mo started to agree, but Trevor put his hand up and stopped him. "Your mouth is full of doughnuts, Mo. Don't talk."

As the two left Ricky Radar asked Trevor if he thought the two would bring the presents to their nieces. There was always the possibility they would try to sell the presents for some cash. Trevor said that there was a good chance that Cindy and Mo would make that delivery. Everyone nodded in agreement. A good chance was good enough.

*****

Chase looked at the letter. "Can I make this delivery? Even if it's just for fifteen minutes, I can play around with this kid."

Dear Santa

I want a bike Please. Cause I have nothing to ride.

I want a friend. Cause I have no one to play with.

I want a skirt for my mom she wears size 18 please.

Sincerely

By Kadeem

Dear Santa
I want a bike Please. Cause I have nothing to ride.
I want a friend cause I have no one to play with.
I want a skirt for my mom she wears size 18 please.
Sincerely
Kadeem

Some children are wise and thoughtful beyond their years. They wish for things because all children do. But this one realizes the stress that Santa must feel—all that burden put on one man's back. So in case he failed to reach her, she knows that even Santa needs unconditional love.

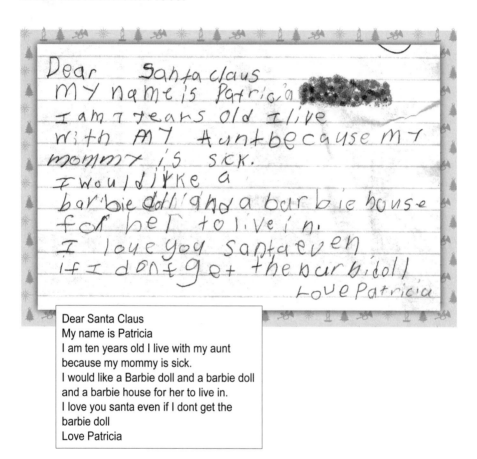

Dear Santa Claus
My name is Patricia
I am ten years old I live with my aunt
because my mommy is sick.
I would like a Barbie doll and a barbie doll
and a barbie house for her to live in.
I love you santa even if I dont get the
barbie doll
Love Patricia

Chapter Twenty-Six

Little Blue Lies

Dave was assigned to the seven-seven for nine months, and left in July of 2003. As always, Dave moved in the direction of becoming a Detective Lieutenant, like Colombo.

Lieutenant Antonio Russo, formerly of the six-seven Detective Squad, was now Captain Russo, in charge of the citywide gun squad. It was a special unit that targeted illegal gun-trafficking in New York City. Russo pulled Dave into his unit. Dave was now living his dream, working as a lieutenant, with detectives. As Dave moved deeper into a world of specialized police-work and highly trained detectives, the only drawback was that his new assignment would pull him away from precinct life.

A lot of people mistakenly think that any officer in plain clothes is an "undercover." Both officers and detectives work in plain clothes for many different reasons. But real *undercovers* infiltrate criminal operations. No one knows them as police officers. True undercover units use real undercover detectives.

While many cops do plain clothes duties, not many can do undercover work. Skill, courage, and an ability to act are needed. Dave worked with some of the best undercover detectives in the business.

✳✳✳✳✳

"Vicky, do you know I work with professional liars?"

"What do you mean Dave?"

"My undercover detectives. Basically, they lie for a living."

"How can you call them liars, Dave? Maybe actors… acting the part of a criminal."

"*Criminal?* I'll tell you criminal. Three-hour lunches. Strange disappearances. Promising me they'll to do last week's paperwork— next week." Dave paused, "I think they do mind control tricks on their sergeant, too."

"I know they exaggerate, Dave. But that's not *criminal.*"

"Oh yeah? How about when they steal every pen I bring into the office—that's petit larceny, a misdemeanor in the penal code."

"Hmmm."

* * * * *

Inside a diner Monty and Chille sat with Dre. Monty, an undercover, wore a leather jacket and baggy jeans. His partner Chille also wore jeans, but hers fit tight, showing off her good shape. She wore a jean jacket over a taut shirt.

They were sitting at the table with a dangerous man. Dre—street name for Andre—passed a briefcase over to Monty. Usually Dre was all over Chille. But today his mind was on something else. His eyes looked more devious than usual.

The package contained the goods. Monty slipped it over to Chille, then passed an envelope back to Dre. With the deal complete, the undercovers started to leave, but Dre wanted to talk. It was bad conversation. Dre looked around as if waiting for something.

The diner was full of people. They were fairly confident that Dre wouldn't try any funny business inside the diner, but they also had no idea who else was around. Monty and Chille made eye contact; they were being set up. Before Dre could put them into a corner they had to make a move.

Chille made a comment about the coffee tasting bad. That was the signal. Their team went into motion.

*****

Inside the diner men at two different tables complained about their coffee too. That was their signal back to Monty and Chille. Outside another backup team was tense and ready. Like coiled springs, some heavily armed detectives sat outside in regular cars, and were ready to jump. In the diner's parking lot Dave nodded to Dee-Dee. She gave a wink back, picked up her cell phone, and made the call.

Inside the diner the Monty looked at his cell phone and *accidentally* answered it with the speaker on. Dre and Chille could hear the girl's voice cleary.

"What's up sugar, wha'cha doing tonight?" It was Dee-Dee's voice.

Monty made a surprised face and turned off the speaker.

"Hey. What's good?" Monte turned away from Chille.

Chille also made a face. But hers was angry. She looked at Monty, and then at Dre. "Oh no he didn't." She pursed her lips and raised her eyebrows. "Do you see this, Dre? My man has got to be out of his mind."

Dre looked back at Chille. He knew Chille and Monty were in a relationship, and it was clear that Monty was speaking to another woman. Dre felt like he was on some reality talk show where the woman starts beating on her unfaithful man.

"Right in front of me!" Chille threw her hands up in the air. Then her hands went to her hips. "Playing me." She shook her head and got up. "I'm outa here."

Dre didn't know what to do. He looked at Monty and pointed to Chille. But Monty pointed to his phone and whispered, "I've got to take this." He mouthed the word "baby" and made a big stomach sign with his hand.

Chille grabbed the package and headed for the door. "All you men are the same," she said.

Dre looked around the diner. People from two different tables gave back questioning looks. The backup cops in the diner saw the exchange of looks, and now knew who Dre's friends were. Monty saw it too. He told Dee-Dee that he got what he needed, and he'd call her back.

Outside the diner Chille got into a livery cab and drove off.

"Good call." Chille said. Dave and Dee-Dee were in the front seat.

Inside the diner Dre asked Monty, "What's up with you and Chille?"

"Just woman stuff. I'll take care of that later. Right now my other girl needs to see me." Monty shrugged his shoulders. Then he said, "Yo, I'm out."

Dre gave Monty's outstretched fist a pound with a fist of his own, and nodded his head. Women troubles came first. Business would have to wait.

*****

Tommy Coughlin was Dave's sergeant. Less than a block away he sat in the back of a delivery van. Two phones and two radios were going all at once. "Scott, Alex, follow those guys by the table next to the window. George, Dean, take that other table. I want the license plates of the cars they get into, and any other car they even look at. Scott and Alex, you keep your eyes on Dre...."

* * * * *

Later Dave sat in the office with his undercovers and the rest of the team. They critiqued the transaction, and everything that had followed. The case detective, Scott Beales had identified more of Dre's associates. There would be more work to do, and more arrests to make when the case was taken down.

"You got the receipt from the diner, Monty?" Dave asked. "For the food, and the gun-transaction, I want my paperwork."

"Boss, we gotta eat first."

"You see what I'm talking about, Tommy?" Dave said to his sergeant. "One hour in the diner and these guys are still talking about getting food. I want my paperwork."

Coughlin nodded in agreement, "Yeah boss, they gotta get that paperwork in."

Monty walked up to Tommy and said, "You see the kind of stress we went through in that diner, Sarge? How we going to eat in there? You know that was some sort of set-up. Now the lieutenant's putting even more pressure on us." Monty walked back and pointed at his supervisors. "You know what? My feelings are hurt."

Tommy nodded in agreement, "Yeah, that work is very stressful. It's crazy out there, who's got time to eat when you're worried about god knows what. I've gotta let you guys relax."

"Don't even start with the nonsense, Monty," Dave said. "For all we know those guys were trying to kidnap you and Chille tonight. I want paper on everything that happened tonight—just in case they try something stupid the next time."

Dave turned to Tommy and said, "How can we build a case with no paperwork? Let's get these guys moving, sergeant."

Tommy got up. "C'mon guys, let's get the paperwork done for the Lieu. You know he's right."

Chille started to walk toward the door. "Me and Dee-Dee gotta get our vitamins, first. You know about that diet we're on, right Lieu?"

Dave walked over to Chille's desk and opened up the middle drawer. He held up four bottles of herbal health. She muttered something under her breath.

"Anybody got a pen?" Dee-Dee asked, sneaking behind Chille towards the locker room.

Dave stopped her and told Scott to pick any of the three jackets on Monty's desk. All the undercovers had thrown their jackets there.

"Any one?" asked Scott.

"Yes. And look in the front pockets."

Scott went into one, then another one, and then the third. He smiled and held up two fistfuls of pens.

Monty started to say something else but stopped. Dave leaned his head forward, half squinted and tensed up the left side of his jaw. His eyes almost started to smoke. Monty knew the look. He had paperwork to do.

* * * * *

Inside our house Dave sat at the table checking over Yumiko's homework. Angelina was putting away her books. Victor was already asleep. In the other room the television speakers announced that American Idol was about to begin. Tomiko looked up and quickly started to pack her books away also.

"Tomiko, is your homework done?"

"Yes Daddy."

"You were just working—you mean you finished all of your homework?" Dave asked.

Tomiko froze.

"*All* of it?" Dave leaned forward and looked at his daughter. The left side of his jaw started to tense up.

"Well not all…."

Angelina put her arm around her little sister and walked her away from their father. "I'll help her finish it Daddy." She told her little sister, "Don't you know you can't lie to Daddy? He's a policeman. People lie to him all day long."

Chapter Twenty-Seven

Kidnapped!

Picture a kidnapping. A van screeches to a halt, cutting the victim off on the sidewalk. Two masked goons get out, place a bag over the victim's head, and throw him into the van. They tie him up with rope, the van drives away, tires smoking and spinning wildly. Got the picture? Okay, this was nothing like that.

When a *cop* gets kidnapped, it's a different story: there's a light tap on his shoulder, and as he turns to see who it is, a hollow feeling takes his breath. Picture being taken by federal agents—dressed in off-beige suits, equipped with no sense of humor, wearing sunglasses when it really isn't that bright out. Actually, that's not strong enough—think of the movie "Men in Black," those special government MIB guys putting their sunglasses on just before they zap your memory with the flash thingy. Hmm, maybe even stronger than that—how about the movie "The Matrix," when the bad guy, agent Smith, smiles cynically at "Neo," and he makes Neo's mouth disappear—get the picture? Because that's the exact helpless feeling you have when investigators from the Internal Affairs Bureau (IAB) approach you, and invite you to come with them. They don't raise their voices. They tell you everything's going to be all right. They ask you to come into their car, and they ask you nicely. They know, and you know, that you can't refuse. In the police department, *that*, my friend, is a *kidnapping*.

*****

It was mid November of 2003. Dave was working in the gun squad where he and his crew were having tremendous success. But Christmas was lurking around the corner and Dave hadn't spent much time in the six-seven or seven-seven during the year. There was no way of knowing if the operation would go forward this year.

Dave tried to get a meeting with his elves, and after a lot of calls and cancellations, he got most of them to agree to meet him after work at a bar in Brooklyn called the Junkyard Dog. Dave hoped that the Blue Christmas could work out this year.

Dave parked his car just outside the station house and got ready to start his work day. No matter what, he thought, he would make the meeting tonight. His sergeants would have to handle whatever came up that day, because he was going to leave work on time.

* * * * *

Dave parked his car and started to walk towards his office, Blue Christmas on his mind. Someone stopped him politely. Too politely.

One of Dave's undercover detectives, Monty, saw Dave getting escorted into a Ford Crown Victoria in the parking lot. Monty called out but all Dave did when he looked back was to shake his head slightly. The IAB captain waved Monty off.

Monty didn't need Dave or the captain to say anything. He knew *exactly* what was happening. And his defensive instincts fired up when that captain waved him off with a cell phone in his hand. He was sure the man was taking pictures of him. Monty wondered, would they take him next? And then who after that? Monty ran up to the office with his coworkers to discuss what had just happened.

* * * * *

During the ride the two investigators from IAB didn't speak much to Dave. This was protocol because they weren't going to discuss the case without the subject's lawyer being present. They spoke to each other in low tones, and the radio, set to country music, was barely audible.

Dave asked his captors if they could turn up the radio's volume. He wasn't a big fan of country, but figured a little music would make the ride more comfortable. When they obliged by turning up the volume, to his surprise, talk radio filled the car. It wasn't a country music station at all. A radio show host was upset because someone had questioned the President about the war. He pointed out that the President's critic had a tarnished record. He did this by shouting this point over and over.

Dave wanted to ask the IAB guys to turn the radio back down, but thought better of it. He didn't want them to think that he was being a wise guy. Instead he turned his head towards the outside and wondered why in the world IAB had grabbed him. What had he done? As a supervisor, Dave knew that he was also responsible for anything done by anyone under him. What could have his men done? He tried to stay calm and not let his mind run away with random scenarios. Eventually his mind drifted back to Blue Christmas. He wondered if he would make his meeting tonight.

* * * * *

The cell phone hot line was in full swing. News of Dave's kidnapping hit the firearms unit hard. It spread to the six-seven squad, and then to six-seven and seven-seven precincts. Elves everywhere were going crazy.

* * * * *

In Brooklyn, there was a bar called the Junkyard Dog where many elves sat waiting. Would the head elf make it to the meeting? They spoke to each other, sharing stories. Although some of the stories were animated and interesting, none of them could be of interest to IAB. So the question remained: what could Dave have done to get kidnapped?

Some of the more senior elves like Trish and Johnny Mack were more positive in their approach. They trusted Dave implicitly. No one could tell them that Dave was in any real trouble, and that everyone there should concentrate on setting up this year's Blue Christmas.

That was when it happened. As the elves started to speak about running the Blue Christmas, they realized that Dave had even a bigger role than they had given him credit for. As they went over the different jobs that Blue Christmas entailed, they saw that it was always Dave who had put the responsibility on his shoulders to get it done. The bottom line was that Dave would always do himself everything that wasn't done—from speaking with schools to chasing Grinches. More than any one of them, Dave just didn't take "no" for an answer.

Blue Christmas had always run well because Dave was there to push it through. Although it was nice to know that everyone jumped onto become elves, taking the helm of the operation was different. It was a lot of work and salesmanship. There was organization and shopping. Missed stops and hurt feelings—neighborhood parents and groups contacting you direct; any and all problems from babies to Grinches sat directly in your lap. And even though Dave loved it all, there were times when even he would throw his hands up... the elves looked at each other, sizing themselves up truthfully. It wouldn't be one on them that would take over the job of being the head elf if Dave stepped down. The elves sat around the bar with a sinking feeling that the Blue Christmas had come to an end.

*****

From inside IAB's Crown Victoria, Dave had watched Monty go into the building. Although he couldn't see him, Dave knew that Monty was somewhere watching. Dave wanted to let his guys know what was happening, but he didn't know himself. Besides, he wouldn't be allowed to go anywhere or call anyone just at that moment.

Chapter Twenty-Eight

Meeting at the Junkyard

After a short, but uncomfortable, ride in a Crown Vic, Dave sat looking around the interview room inside the internal affairs office. "Sparse," was the word that best described the small room. A table with no drawers, four chairs, a tape recorder.

The two IAB investigators just outside the door went about their business as if Dave wasn't there. Dave tried to stretch out, but the room was small, and there was no give in his wooden chair. He still felt crammed in. So this is what it feels like to be kidnapped, he thought. Not knowing why, was the most fearful thing of all.

* * * * *

The internal affairs bureau investigated all allegations of corruption. They were the police that policed the police. Most of their investigations ended with an official inquiry. Although both investigators didn't think the Blue Christmas was an IAB matter, once a case was given to them, they had to follow protocol to the letter.

"At the times in question, lieutenant, did you get a quantity of teddy bears at a discounted price?" the IAB captain asked Dave.

An IAB lieutenant sat next to the captain, and Dave's lawyer sat next to Dave. There was no one else in the room besides these four, and the interview was being recorded on tape.

"Yes sir, I did," Dave answered.

"Did you get the discount because you work for the NYPD, lieutenant?"

"No sir. Mr. Smith gives discounts to many different charities. He gave me a good price because his bears were going to the neighborhood children."

"I see."

The captain and lieutenant both scribbled away on the papers in front of them.

"Next question: did you ever threaten to hit anyone with a "Grinch" list?"

"To hit them, or hit them with the *list*?"

Both IAB men looked at each other. They nodded of agreement, "Yes."

Dave looked at his lawyer, who raised his eyebrows.

Without waiting for an answer, the IAB captain continued with the questioning, "And for the record, lieutenant, just what kind of weapon is this Grinch list?"

＊＊＊＊＊

The Junkyard Dog was full of elves that had gotten there early. Speculation was the topic of every discussion. Would Dave make the meeting? What was it that he had actually done? Did Internal Affairs know that they had kidnapped their Blue Christmas?

The meeting was supposed to start at eight o'clock, and every elf had come on time. Dave's habit with cops was to call all meetings one hour earlier then he expected to arrive, knowing that it would still take another half hour to get the meeting started. To every elf's surprise Dave walked in the Junkyard Dog at 9 o'clock. To Dave's surprise *all* his elves were already there.

Dave's best undercover detective, Monty, walked up to Dave first. Dave could see that Monty was ready to go out on the town after the meeting because he was dressed up in his favorite dress clothes: a purple zoot-suit with black pinstripes.

"Hey Lieutenant—did you escape? What happened? I was thinking of trying to get the guys from our office to tail you, but those IAB guys got you out of there quick."

"Thanks Monty, that's why I always count on you," Dave answered.

"Aw don't be sarcastic, El-Tee, you know I wouldn't let nobody take you other than the NYPD—if it was the Mafia or the Feds, or something—it would have been on!" Monty patted the waist area of his zoot-suit where he held his gun was and nodded at Dave. "You know I got you."

"Yes, I know you got me, Monty. Thank you." This time Dave was being sincere. Although Monty tended to exaggerate, he was an undercover detective who put himself in dangerous situations almost on a daily basis. An, "I got you," from a man like this was no small gesture.

Dave smiled and gave Monty a hug. Monty grinned. He turned to the rest of the bar and threw his hands in the air, victoriously.

Trevor walked up to Dave and said, "Where did you go after they took you? And can you talk about it? Monty says that a couple of other cars followed your car out."

Dave shook his head. He could only imagine the stories Monty had put out.

* * * * *

"I don't know anything about other cars, I just went to the IAB office for official questioning. It turned out to be about Blue Christmas."

"IAB *investigated* Blue Christmas?" At least ten of the elves asked the same question at once, and it was then echoed by all the rest.

"They investigate all allegations," Dave replied. "Discounted teddy bears, shaking down Grinches, whatever—it's their job."

After a few headshakes, Johnny Mack asked the obvious, "So someone *called* IAB about Blue Christmas and reported you for getting free teddy bears? Who would do that?"

"*Discounted* teddy bears," Dave replied. "And if some Grinch called IAB, it doesn't matter, because the IAB guys did their job and it's over. What matters now is if we do a Blue Christmas this year or not."

Dave's elves were relieved with the bottom line, that Dave wasn't in trouble. And if IAB had conducted an investigation into the matter, then Blue Christmas was officially in the clear.

Drinks, cop and Christmas stories were on the menu for the rest of the night. A few Brooklyn elves rallied around the good news and all promised to do a Blue Christmas in the six-seven and seven-seven for the Christmas of 2003.

Chapter Twenty-Nine

Blue On Its Own

The Junkyard Dog meeting had produced two new head elves who promised to do their best to keep the Blue Christmas going for the year of 2003. For the six-seven and seven-seven, the familiar operation would be in full effect.

In the seven-seven Captain Christina Hamilton became the head elf. She had witnessed the operation the year before. She had no problem being the front person.

To Dave she resembled a Mrs. Clause. She was in her mid-forties, had a bit of white hair, a little roundish. She laughed easily and loudly. The big glasses she wore softened her face. Although she was a captain, she was very approachable.

In the six-seven, the head elf was Sergeant Dwight Schroeder. He was the administrative sergeant of the six-seven. He was a man who preferred to stay behind the scenes. He put envelopes into each sergeant's mailbox along with a list of their personnel. He typed up instructions for the school sergeants. He neatly checked off his "to-do" lists. But he wasn't "hands-on" like Dave was. He didn't understand that police-elves could get a little lazy, and needed to be roughed-up at times.

*****

Dave wondered if the years past had taken their effect. Like himself, many officers in both precincts had moved on. Johnny Mack was upstairs with the detectives; Chase became an undercover in the narcotics division; Rex decided to become a fireman like his father. This was always the case in the police department—lots and lots of movement.

But many of the cops had also stayed. Trish, Trevor and Ricky Radar were still there. So was Nick Adams and Kenny Martin.. Dave knew that the true measure of success would be an Operation: Blue Christmas going forward without him.

*****

The two new head elves weren't tornados. They weren't even rough storms. But they were proficient cops, and they did get the job done. Shortages and all, the year of 2003 sported a Blue Christmas in both the six-seven and seven-seven.

The deliveries of 2003 were made in the six-seven and seven-seven again.

*****

Ever wonder what the perfect gift is? Sometimes 'useful' can replace 'flashy' or 'fun.'

Dear Santa,
How are you?
My name is Ashley
I am 7 year old.
I would like a book bag.
Merry Christmas!
Your Friend
Ashley

Captain Christina Hamilton came into the seven-seven precinct with two armfuls of book bags. When Dave asked her what she had, she said, "Necessities, I thought. But apparently they're luxuries. I never knew so many kids didn't have book bags."

She saw Dave about to speak but she cut him off. "Don't even look at me like that, lieutenant. I don't care about your five-dollar limit. I make a captain's salary and I'll buy what I damn please."

"Yes ma'am."

Dear Santa,

I wish that I could have two learning books so I could learn more. I want one book to teach me about adjectives, verbs, and nouns. The other book is to teach me how to do math problems.
Love,
Shenelle

It would make Christmas shopping so much easier if every kid could somehow combine their wishes for presents with the need to get things that are useful.

The squad detectives got into the delivery act in the six-seven. Johnny Mack had made it upstairs to the squad. He was used to delivering for Blue Christmas, so he got some detectives to help him out.

For the task of delivering presents, they were a "crusty" pair to say the least: senior detectives, Red and Little Bob. Knowledgeable investigators, hardened faces—now surrounded by toys in the muster room of the six-seven. They picked up toys and teddy bears and looked at them like they were evidence.

"Little" Bob Slayton and Mark "Red" Redding, with a total of fifty-three years of combined police service, looked at a letter to Santa. Both stared at the letter for a while as Red held it out with both hands.

Red's cigarette bounced up and down on his lip as he read the letter. Little Bob's head nodded in rhythm with the cigarette. In his hand, Little Bob held an empty plastic bag.

"Adrian?" Red asked Little Bob, "that a boy's name, or a girl's?"

Little Bob thought for a minute. "I think it can be both," he said.

"Oh." Now Red stopped to think for a minute. "Better be prepared for either, right?"

Little Bob nodded in agreement, and they put a boy's and a girl's present into the plastic bag.

"What if there's a sister there?" Red asked his partner. "That we don't know about, Little Bob."

"Yeah Red, lot of sisters out there. Better get more stuff. We don't want to get caught short. We'd have to make a second trip, Red."

"Yeah Little Bob. We don't want to have to make a second trip."

Red and Little Bob looked at the toys around the room. But neither moved. "What if it's a younger sister, Little Bob?"

"Younger?"

"Yeah, younger. Or maybe older. What do you think Little Bob?"

"Yeah Red, lot of sisters, lot of ages. Could be an older *and* a younger sister there." Little Bob scratched his head. "Or two younger sisters… better to just get more stuff, Red."

"Yeah, Little Bob. You've got a point there."

The two looked around, and again, did not move.

"Hey Red?" Little Bob asked, "what if there's a little brother there…"

* * * * *

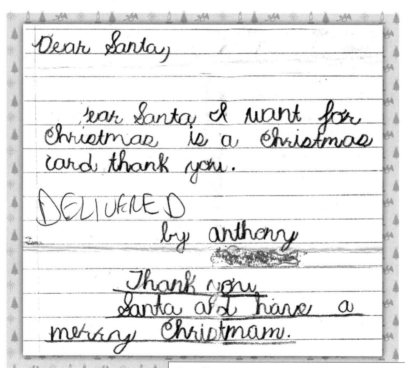

Dear Santa,
Dear Santa I want for Christmas is a Christmas card thank you.
by Anthony
Thank you
Santa and have a merry Christmas

Officer Damian Doyle came into the seven-seven with a couple of gifts under his arm.

"This one, Lieu—I got this one."

Dave looked at the officer, who was obviously angry.
"No problem. What do you have there?"

"These are presents, that's okay, right Lieu? I'll give one of your small gifts if you want, but I'm going to give this kid something on my own."

"Okay, but why are people yelling at me today?"

"Do you know what my nephews asked me for this Christmas? Do you think they gave one thought about me this year, other than what I might bring them? And this kid's asking for a Christmas card? I think I'll spend a few dollars on someone who'll appreciate a present. Thank you for asking, Lieutenant."

Dave backed up with his hands up. "You got it, officer. It's your show."

Dave had never heard Damian ever raise his voice before this day. He saw how the officer's eyes had welled up with tears at the thought of a child asking for nothing more than a Christmas card. Although the officer felt embarrassed, Dave respected him that much more.

A teacher's red pen highlighted a family's plight. Judging by the strong penmanship, Dave figured that it was the teacher's black pen that had written the letter.

Dear Santa,
My name is Stephanie I am 10 years old.
On nov.16,2003 My family and I suffered
a fire. I would like to receive anything that
involves with SpongeBob.
Thanking you Kindly
Stephanie
P.S. I am currently staying with a friend.

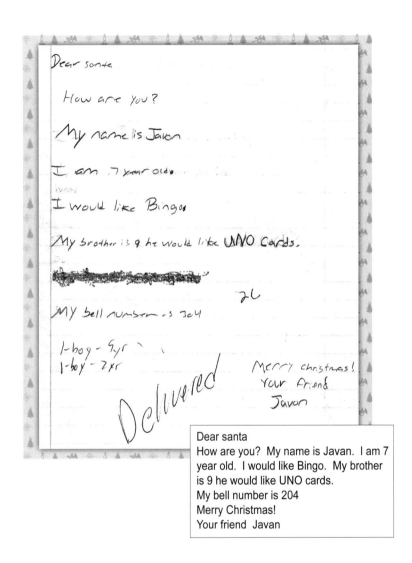

Dear santa
How are you? My name is Javan. I am 7 year old. I would like Bingo. My brother is 9 he would like UNO cards.
My bell number is 204
Merry Christmas!
Your friend Javan

Officer Joe Marciano stared and stared at the letter. Not knowing what else to say, Dave asked him if he was all right.

Marciano replied, "I'm not sure, Lieu. I've been working this precinct for years… this kid's not asking for much at all. I just feel like I'm seeing this place for the first time."

*****

184

Did you ever just wonder? Feel the need to just take a walk to get your head straight? Sometimes kids need to do the same. Wonder about the weather, what clothes to wear… things like that.

Dear Santa,
How are your elves? I was wondering if you could help me out getting something since its' getting cold and all. I really need a pair of gloves you would make me happy
from
Horasha
PS
Say Hi to Mr.s Santa

Dear Santa,
My family is having trouble getting things. I was wondering if you can get my cousin a jacket and some gloves because she has been wandering around thinking about getting a jacket. tell mrs clause I said Hi and have a happy new year.
Love Shante
P.S. miss you

Note the "P.S."

Chapter Thirty

Stepping Back

In 2004, Dave's tireless work ethic helped get him far in the police department. But his hard-headedness also made him stand out too.

Dave stood in an office with of piles of guns all around. His Detectives wrote notes on vouchers. They were getting ready to take down a group of illegal gun-traffickers, and the take-down of this case would hit the press. Over one-hundred guns, rifles, and machine guns would be put on display, and once the press conference was over, each voucher would have to be redone so the guns could be used for evidence. The preparation for an hour press conference would take a squad of detectives a good many hours.

But Dave's concerns went beyond the press conference. Captain Antonio Russo had gotten promoted and moved on, leaving Dave with a new captain in charge. Captain Krum was a different man with a different style. Dave held a telephone about a foot from his ear as his new boss screamed away. When he stopped Dave answered.

"You've got the paperwork for that, Captain, I e-mailed you that to you." Dave held the phone away from his ear again and made a face while his detectives giggled and pointed at him.

"No Capt, that's the other case with the murder suspect, you have that report on your desk, I faxed it to you last week three times." Dave paused and again held the phone away. "No Capt, I have no idea what your desk looks like."

While the setting up of the third press conference case of the year might sound glamorous, the reality is that each case came with tons of work; and Dave's boss, Captain Krum, was getting hit with questions from his superiors. Press conference cases were the kind of thing that brought the department magnifying glass onto a unit.

Krum's mind, and his desk, was covered with notes and reminders of which chief to call back with what information. He was a man who was overwhelmed. He wanted the accolades that came with being in the NYPD's top gun squad, but had no idea about the work that came along with being number one. All Krum knew that every time he spoke to a chief, they were going to ask him more questions, and demean him when he didn't have the exact answers they wanted. Krum started to feel that Dave's squad, doing so many cases that were worthy of press, was driving him into an early grave.

Krum called Dave about nineteen times a day, screaming questions and demanding reports. Dave saw this as an attempt to slow him down, and being hard-headed, picked the pace up every time.

*****

It was an early September afternoon. After a successful press conference, the guys were ready to go out for some food and drink, which Dave knew would last well into the night. Dave opted to pass, and finally make a parents-teachers conference, scheduled for early that evening. On the way home he stopped in a Brooklyn boxing gym.

Bedford-Stuyvesant Boxing had been home to two world champion boxers in their youth—Mark Breland and Riddick Bowe. But the heyday of Bed-Stuy had long moved on. Now it was a run down gym, fighting for survival. A couple of dedicated trainers were the only thing keeping the gym from closing. They had vowed to give some of the tougher kids an alternative to the streets, and boxing was what they knew. Dave had known the trainers, Charles, Clarence and Nate for years, but never found the time to come to the gym steady. Today was a good day for a visit.

"We keep telling you Dave, just come in, just work out," Nate said in his deep voice with a southern accent. "These kids need another look in here—the police would be good for them."

Over the years Dave had spoken to Nate about having the police boxing team work out at this gym. It was at a good location, centrally located, and as for Nate, he had seen too many kids go off in the wrong direction. He felt cops in his gym would be a good look; Nate wanted his gym to have a positive effect on the kids.

"Yo Junior, Roy—come here!" Nate called a couple of teens over. "This here is Lieutenant Dave, from the police department. He's going to show you two some drills—work with him."

Dave saw a look flash over the kids' faces when Nate said "police" but what a boxing coach says is what goes, and the kids offered no resistance. At first it was awkward for Dave, but after taking off his jacket and tie, he had the kids working well. With the right mixture of challenges, a few words of selective encouragement, the two kids were throwing good punch combinations and making defensive moves as they darted back and forth. Dave was swinging a towel at first, making sure the kids understood that defense always followed offense, and soon Dave had on a pair of gloves so the kids could move out the way of real punches, as they practiced theirs.

Out of breath, Dave came back to Nate after three rounds.

"Not quite in shape, Dee?" Nate smiled, "These kids will get you back you know."

As Dave nodded, Nate pointed to the side. To Dave's surprise there was a line of kids waiting for him to work the drills that he had showed

Junior and Roy. Charles and Clarence were laughing, "Can't stop yet, Dave. That wouldn't be fair to these guys!"

Dave knew he couldn't leave. So in a warm day in September, his suit pants and dress shirt got all sweaty, as a bunch of kids from Bed-Sty worked some new drills with delight.

As Dave thanked the coaches and turned to leave, Clarence said something to a kid that made Dave stop.

"You liked those policeman's drills, didn't you son?"

"Yes!"

"Didn't know there's some policeman that know about boxing, huh?"

"Those drills were great, Clarence."

"Yeah Lieutenant Dave gave you guys a little gift today, looks like Christmas came early!"

* * * * *

After the parents-teachers conference Dave worked with our children on homework. Dave was especially good at math, and was a little dismayed that his kids didn't seem to share his natural inclination. He worked with them for hours, making them miss their favorite TV shows.

That night I expected to hear all about the press conference, but instead Dave was all about math and Bed-Stuy boxing. To say he had trouble sleeping that night was an understatement. Getting up to fix the blankets and pillows, or going to get a drink of water, several times, and then later to go to the bathroom, again, several times. When he started to do sit-ups on the floor at four in the morning, I had to protest.

Dave agreed, and came to bed. But before I drifted off to sleep, I saw him lying awake; his eyes reflecting the green light of the neon clock, looking far beyond our bedroom ceiling.

Chapter Thirty-One

Life Happens

Another year in the gun squad put Dave further out of touch with his two favorite precincts. Many of the old faces had been replaced. He and his gun team had spent the year's days and nights running through New York City searching for guns, stopping violence.

Captain Christina Hamilton was transferred out of the seven-seven. She now worked in the Bronx. Sergeant Dwight Schroeder just had new baby twins. He came into work half asleep. Dave had fewer people to turn to for help. As Christmas of 2004 drew nearer, Dave worried.

Dave couldn't find someone to volunteer as a point person in either precinct. All of his elves were happy to help—but taking the lead role was another matter. They all had seen what kind of work it entailed.

Blue Christmas was no ordinary operation, and it needed someone with a peculiar blend of qualities to keep it going. The person had to have the right mix of determination, charm, and *madness*. And they had to be just mean enough in the right places to make things work. Meanwhile, Christmas loomed nearer.

*****

"I don't think it's going to go this year, Vicky. There have been too many changes."

"Don't say that Dave, you've always come through."

"That's the point, Vicky. I'm not there any more. It's not up to me.

I can't be the point person anymore, and I didn't do a good enough job of replacing myself."

"Can't you go to the precincts yourself?"

"Yeah, but there are so many new people. You know how it is." Dave thought for a second. "It isn't fun hitting people you don't know. I can't go around just punching and mugging strangers, Vicky. Even if they are cops."

"Hmmm."

* * * * *

As he had done the year before Dave called a meeting at the Junkyard Dog at eight o'clock. The meeting started promptly at nine-thirty.

All the senior elves were there. Johnny Mack, now a detective in the six-seven squad, respected senior officers Trevor and Ricky Radar, Chase, an undercover detective, Kenny Martin and Nick Adams, both detectives in warrant squads, and Trish, now married, was seven months pregnant with her first child.

Although the topic was supposed to be Blue Christmas, the old friends talked mostly about their lives and what they were doing. Stories of work, and Christmases past brought up both tears and smiles. Without saying it, everyone knew that they had all moved on, and onto the new stories that were now filling their lives.

Finally Trish asked the question, "Will you do the Blue Christmas this year, Dave?"

Dave looked at his friends and smiled. He knew that none of his elves would take the top elf position that was required for a successful Blue Christmas.

Johnny Mack read Dave's eyes and said, "It doesn't have to be an all-out operation Dave, you could scale it down."

Instead of answering, Dave smiled and looked at his drink.

"Nah," Trevor said, "Dave's not like that. It's all or nothing. It's done right or it's not done at all, isn't that so, Dave?"

Dave looked around and exchanged nods with all his elves. And just like that, the Blue Christmas had come to an end.

But Trish, now with the elevated understanding of a mother-to-be, saw something besides the end.

"Will you do something else, Dave?" Trish asked.

＊＊＊＊＊

At home that night I asked my husband the same question that Trish had asked earlier. There was a thought floating around in his head that was just beneath the surface.

"There are plenty of things for me to do, dear." He said, "Christmas Day and Christmas Eve are only two days out of the year. Maybe it's time for me to get into gear."

"Get into gear? Don't you do enough, Dave?"

"Maybe I should be working with kids, Vicky. The NYPD is a big department. There's stuff like the PAL, maybe I should be working that."

Dave's dream was to be the same rank as Colombo. He had a good shot at that in the gun squad.

"What about becoming a Detective Lieutenant, Dave?"

"I don't know. Maybe the gun thing isn't the right place for me. I'm running around the city chasing after bad guys which is fun, but I feel like I'm missing out on our kids growing up. I'm also out of touch with the guys in the precincts, and the boxing gym—I just feel off-base."

As his wife I knew first hand that Dave felt a little off-base—running cases with his undercover teams had overwhelmed other parts of his life. Although he was a man with a dream, he was still a man. Someone who enjoyed his family, and who appreciated the different aspects in his life. Losing the Blue Christmas hit home, and Dave could see that he was losing other things as well. Over the years Dave had always felt that he received more from the Blue Christmas than any effort he put in. Now, this insight on his own life would be Blue Christmas' final gift to Dave.

"I don't know Vicky, maybe working with programs where cops and kids do stuff together—maybe that's for me.

"What did your elves say about that?"

"Get this—they said it would be like Blue Christmas everyday."

"And what about you, Dave, and the promotion you've worked so hard for?"

"I've worked some serious cases that most Detective Lieutenants never had a chance to work. What's meant to be is meant to be."

I could see Dave's mind was made up again. Again, I wasn't exactly sure of what. I didn't mind though, the gun stuff was so dangerous. After all, I am a wife.

"You know what they never show on those Colombo shows, Dave?"

"What's that, Vicky?"

"His children."

* * * * *

A group of people could stay together only for a certain amount of time, and the memories they make is the story they share. That night in bed, Dave and I spoke about the end of Blue Christmas and then about all of the changes going on in everyone's lives. In our own lives, we tried to remember our best friends growing up, and our school buddies through the years, who we loved to work with, and so on. I wondered about my childhood friends in Cuba and Dave tried to count how many cousins he had in different countries.

"Isn't it funny how it happens, Dave?"

"What's that dear?"

"Life."

"Life happens, Vicky?"

"Yes, life *does* happen. And then we all move on."

Chapter Thirty-Two

The Last Secret

Some secrets are confidential. Other secrets are really the main ingredient. Like health is the *secret* of happiness, or hard work is the *secret* of success.

The doubts in your mind can tell you about the hundred things that may go wrong. But in your heart you feel what's right. The secret of doing something special is nothing more than knowing when to follow your heart instead of your mind. The reward for doing this is something that you can never touch, but a magic that you will always feel.

*****

On Christmas Eve of 2004, Dave found himself on the sidelines. He pulled out his letters and looked through them, as he had always done. I sat down next to him and as I always did, asked him about the little girl, had he ever seen her again? The answer was no, but by the way Dave paused, I knew he always wished her well. Dave's Blue Christmas policy was to never look for any of the kids, and that the givers of the gifts shouldn't look for thanks, or anything else. Giving a small gift didn't give anyone the right to infringe on anyone else's life.

Although the Blue Christmas was over, Dave went through his letters anyway, as was his habit over the last few years. As he did, he held onto one a little bit longer, and smiled.

"What is that, Dave?" I asked

"One of my many motivators, right here, Vicky. One of the secrets that kept me going."

I looked at the letter. "This one?"

"Yes indeed."

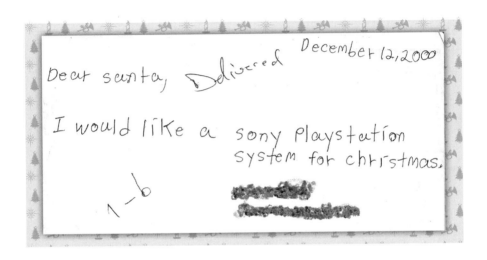

When I looked at the letter I remembered how Dave would get frustrated because of how he made it clear to the teachers that he could only get small gifts for the children. I remembered his first, and only, trip to the post office as well. But knowing that Dave kept this particular in his secret pile, I asked him to tell me about it.

Dave explained to me how Officer Eason B. Barnes had come up to him one day, about a week after Christmas. He gave Dave back his letter.

Eason had a big, meaty grin that could melt ice. There was no cop in the six-seven friendlier. He approached Dave, grabbed his hand, and shook it up and down.

"Thanks Sarge. You made my day."

Dave had given out a lot of letters, and forgotten which one he had given to Eason. But he knew if he had given it to Eason B. Barnes personally, it had to be a special delivery. Trying to figure out which letter it was, Dave asked how the delivery went.

"The kid was kind of upset at first, because it wasn't exactly what he asked for, but you know it was a nice toy—a racing car set, and he did admit that he liked it." Eason said.

"So what else did you tell him?" Dave asked.

"Well I told him that Santa can't be everywhere and that sometimes he might use people like us in the NYPD, to help out."

"Great Eason, you're a good elf. Did you tell him that it was a special delivery?"

"Oh yes. I told him that Santa directed us special to go see him. I didn't tell him that Santa was you, Sarge. Anyway, the kid started jumping up and down and yelling at his cousin. You see, Santa *isn't* dead! Santa isn't dead!"

"The boy said Santa isn't dead?"

"Well his cousin told him that Santa was dead."

"That's a little harsh, no?"

"It was." Eason said it with a straight face, but immediately broke back into his signature grin. "But now, with the present, he could tell his cousin that Santa wasn't dead—and that made my day!"

* * * * *

"So this letter is from that day?" I asked.

"Yes it is."

"This is one of your *secrets*, Dave, that kept you going?"

"Yup, because you can't quit when you know you're right."

I looked at the letter again, and thought about the story he just told me.

"Hmmm, I don't quite get it, Dave."

Dave looked at me, and then at the letter folded in my hands. "You're holding it wrong, Vicky. You have to open it up, dear."

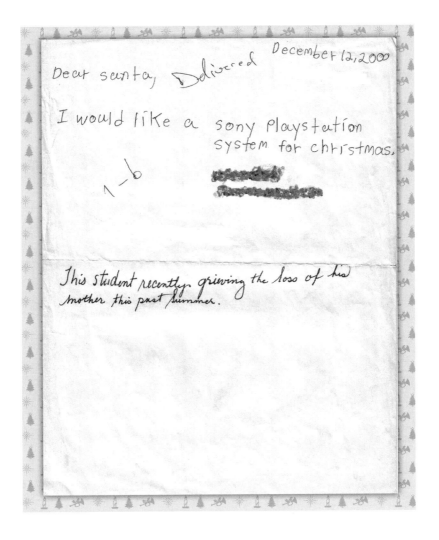

And when I did, I understood.

"Yes, Dave, I see it clearly now."

Last Blue Christmas Lesson

_____

_____

_____

_____

(Left blank for the reader to fill in.)

The End

ABOUT THE AUTHORS

Victoria Siev was born in Cuba and immigrated to the United States with her family as a little girl. She grew up in Brooklyn where her mother and father lived their version of the American Dream by working hard. Victoria got her college degree from New York City Technical Colege and worked in different fields before coming onto the police force. She is now a retired NYPD Police Officer. Her devotions include her husband Dave, and their four children: Angelina, Tomiko, Yumiko, and Victor.

Dave Siev is a Japanese-Jewish American, with a Lithuanian decent. At the time of publication he has served nineteen years in the NYPD. He has been the President and coach of the NYPD Fighting Finest Boxing team for nine years; and has worked in many different units within the police force. One of his notable accomplishments was working as the head supervisor on the largest gun-trafficking case in the history of the NYPD.